TALES

by

10

Tales by 10
Copyright 2018

ISBN
978-0-9978245-6-8 Tales by 10 Print
978-0-9978245-7-5 Tales by 10 ePub

Published by

il fennore publishing
il-fennore-pub.com

Title by Charlie Wyatt
Cover Photo by J.E. Michals
Book Design by Gerry Strong

Other Writers Speak...

"This anthology is a perfect example of literary talent and new ideas coming together to add to the art of writing. A wonderful opportunity to read promising writers who will soon make their mark in the world of literature." **Mark Carlson,** CL, ACS, Author, *The Marines' Lost Squadron – The Odyssey of VMF-422.*

"If you read only one anthology this spring, this should be it. It covers the spectrum from fantasy to terror and has some fine poems as well." **Robert Pacilio,** Author: *Meetings at the Metaphor Café, Midnight Comes to the Metaphor Café,* and *The Restoration.*

"An insightful and thought-provoking anthology that touches the heart and frees the mind." **Colleen J. Pallamary,** Author of *Scammunition, The Vampire Preservation Society,* and *Meet Bridgeport's Sweetheart, Colleen J. Bartram.*

"You'll find these stories and poems engaging, entertaining, encouraging, and ofttimes challenging.You'll be fascinated and surprised. You may become a slightly different person after spending some time in the company of these writers and their work." **Ronald Pickett** – Veterans' Writing Group: Writer/ Producer, *Away for the Holidays, Listen Up!*

CONTRIBUTOR'S PAGE

Compiling this anthology has been particularly challenging. How does any editor select the best work from a group of writers who are continually and regularly published? The number of tales grew weekly.

To get out in front of this issue, our editors camped out at Storytellers' Collaborative, the Read and Critique Group that holds this writing tribe together. Easier? Yes. But keep in mind these writers have been published thirteen straight months in diverse publications: *Chicken Soup for the Soul, Tell Us a Story, Dead Mule School of Southern Literature, Saturday Evening Post, Stoneslide Corrective, Sun Magazine, Audible, Thema Literary Magazine, The Foreign Service Journal,* and numerous anthologies relating military experiences.

Many Storytellers' Collaborative writers are poets as well. This meant our editors winnowed through poetry publications by the hundreds: *Baseball Bard, The Journal of Contemporary Poets, San Diego Poetry Annual, Milkweed, Poetry USA,* and other well-established journals to select the best of the best. Keep in mind four group members have published books; one has been published over 400 times! So, fueled by coffee—lots of coffee—Gold Fish crackers, and chocolates, our readers persisted. The result is a book crammed with high-quality prose and poetry.

These tales embrace life. They illustrate love. They tell of failures. They speak of joy, sing of victory. They bruise, anger, entertain. Hopefully, they'll even change a viewpoint or two, or maybe deliver a new perception along the way.

Charlie Wyatt tweaks your heart with Zeke's return to his hometown, Toadvine, Alabama, after serving in the first Gulf War. Charlie also gives us a different view of a silver-screen hero with "Then I Said to John Wayne..." Charlie's characters seep into your memory with humor and pathos.

One of **Marlys Collom's** poems is never enough. Her offerings create order from chaos, extract reality from dire circumstances, make us cry and laugh and frolic. And think. Her poetry opens hearts and minds.

Michele Ivy Davis' writings explore people, incidents, everyday situations. Her stories smack you in the center of this thing called life and provide insights that linger long after you lay down the book.

Judy Opdycke's pen is sharp. Entertaining. She'll introduce you to complex, yet delightful, folks you wished lived next door. Or not. This wordsmith's plots turn, zig-zag, and wallop hard.

Like mystery? **Gerry Strong's** chapter books about ace mystery-solver, Charlotte, a pug, teach, entertain, and delight. Adults, too, find her work magical. She felt honored when she heard one of her books helped a child learn to read.

Want to ride a dragon? Wield a short sword? **Peter Cruikshank** invites you to visit his world of fantasy, where Julia discovers truth through her dreams. You'll share her fears, be inspired by her courage, and enjoy her heart-stopping adventures.

Elisa Blaisdell's word skills scathe. They entertain. Clarify. Her classic short story, "To the Rocks," set in ancient times, delivers truths for today. She explores aging, relationships, and reality in a layered, haunting fashion that will be long remembered.

Enjoy the feeling of righteousness when justice prevails? The protagonists in **J. E. Michals'** books transition quickly from quiet existence into justified violence. Trouble—figuratively—comes visiting. Trouble should have stayed home.

R. Boyd Palmer has spent a lifetime crafting words—spoken and written—as an actor and poet. His poems are musical. Lyrical. Muscular. Did I say romantic? You'll say "Thank you" after his words rip at your heart with new concepts and viewpoints.

Pete Peterson's stories are as subtle as a bare-knuckle punch to the gut. His "Winner Take All" features guts and gore where the winning fighter takes home the pot, yet finds rewards greater than money. Like a team of mules or the loser's wife.

Each writer in this closely-curated work displays an abundance of talent, skill, and devotion to their craft. This anthology proves they deserve a larger role in the pantheon of American writers.

TABLE OF CONTENTS

TABLE OF CONTENTS

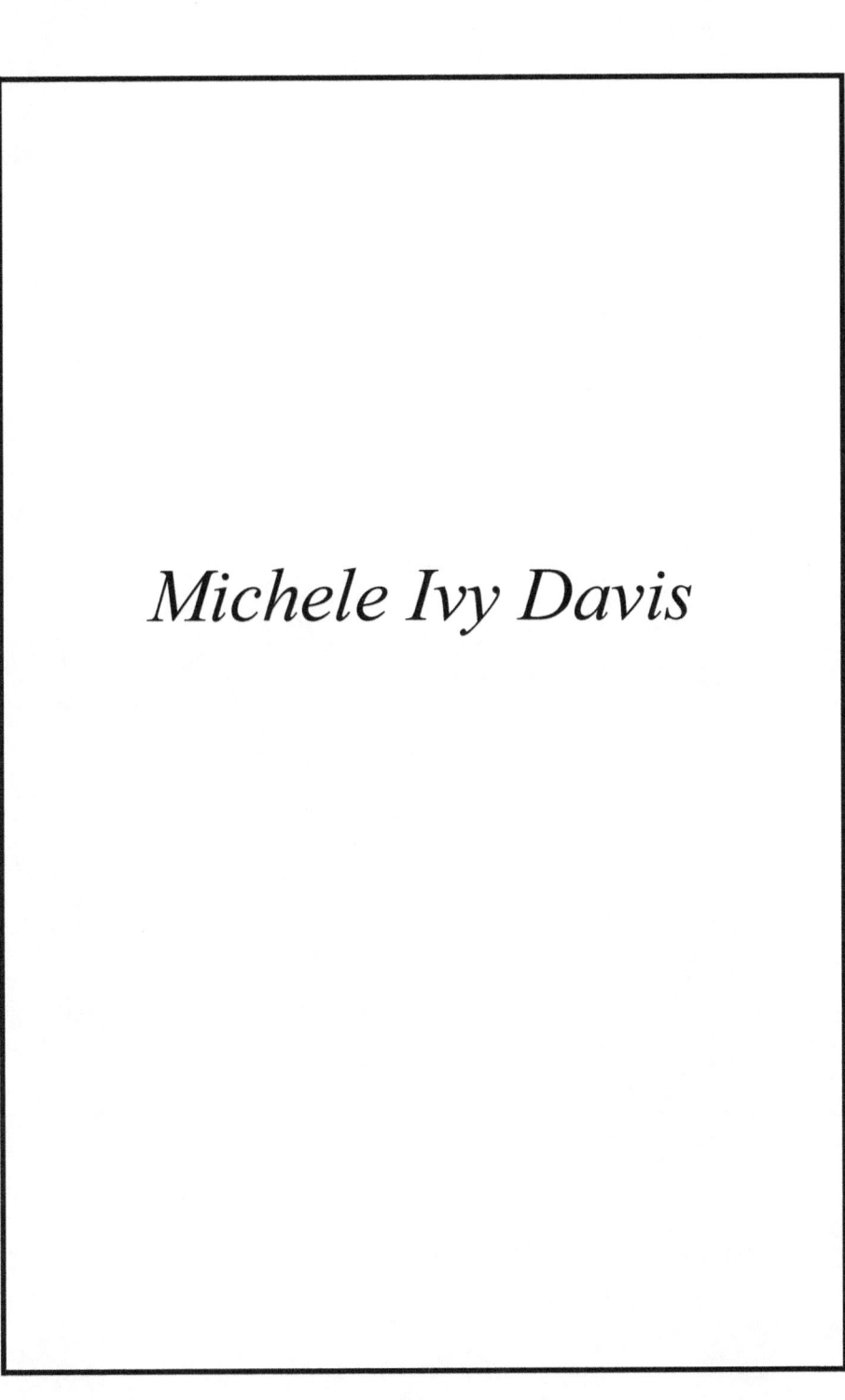

Michele Ivy Davis

THE WISH BOOK

The fat Sears Catalog was called "The Wish Book" by many in those days. It had over 1,000 pages of the necessities and luxuries of life: everything from bunk beds to bicycles, waffle irons to well pumps. But to my younger sister and me, it was so much more. It was our connection with all things American—with ready-made clothes, American styles, and with a life that was passing us by, half a world away.

As I graduated from elementary school, my Foreign Service family was sent to its first post overseas. We were stationed in Madras (now Channai), a small seaport town on the southeast coast of India. It was the 1950's—a time of propeller planes and ship travel. Television had not yet come to that country and phone calls across the ocean were not yet possible. Communication with "the States" was by letter or telegram. When conditions were right, we could get "Your Hit Parade" on the short wave radio, but it came on at three in the morning. Even American music was not part of our everyday life.

Most of our clothes were made by a tailor because there weren't any dress shops selling European-style clothes. Even our shoes were made by a shoemaker, although after he made a pair of loafers for my sister that looked exactly like the catalog picture but made her look like she had giant clown feet, we gave up on that.

The Sears Roebuck and Montgomery Ward catalogs became our lifeline to our homeland. My mother would prop the big book on the coffee table, opening it to the page that told how to determine clothing

1

sizes. She would study the drawings, then follow the instructions, measuring our arms, necks, backs and legs carefully with a tape measure. Finally, she would get out pieces of white paper and a pencil, and carefully trace around our stocking feet to send with the shoe order. How it tickled! After having us try on clothes of various sizes from friends, recording our latest measurements, and relying on her intuition, she would do her best to guess how big we would be when the clothes arrived three months later—not an easy task with rapidly-growing early teenagers.

Meanwhile, my sister, Diane, and I would pore over the catalog, picking out first what we needed and then what we would like to have, staying within the boundaries our mother had set. Shipping was expensive so we had to be careful. When the order was finally written, sealed, and mailed, we would wait as it went around the world to Sears or Wards, where it would be filled and sent back to us by sea.

At last the ship would arrive with our order and the package delivered to my father's office. We were always excited when he brought it home, but he and my mother would whisk it into their bedroom and firmly close the door, leaving us in the hall. We would wait impatiently as they removed secret birthday presents and Christmas gifts. Finally they would allow us to come into the room. On the bed was the wonderful box, packing paper scattered, and clothes folded very flat, smashed from their many months' journey to us.

We never knew what we were going to get until the box arrived. Sometimes items were out of stock. In an early order, only one of us got a jacket to wear in the chilly evenings at the boarding school we attended in the hills. Sometimes the stores substituted something "similar," although we did not consider the box of clove Life Savers a fair substitution for the fruit-flavored ones my mother had ordered as a treat. When the style of shoes I had chosen arrived in my sister's size and hers in mine, I knew that they could also make mistakes.

Periodically, by the time the clothes arrived we had outgrown them. In a letter from boarding school, I told my mother that my younger sister's new shoes were "way too small. She could get her foot into them, but she looked like one of the stepsisters trying to fit her foot into Cinderella's glass slipper." My new shoes were also too small. Since they fit my sister, I gave them to her; I had my old shoes resoled.

When items were too small, we usually turned them over to someone else in the American community, but we hated to do that. We had waited three months for them, and disliked the fact that someone else would get to wear "our" new clothes. When things were too big, I often wore them at school anyway, taking them in where needed with an inexperienced needle and thread.

But things didn't always go wrong; sometimes when things arrived, they were perfect. In one of those perfect orders, we each got an entire outfit—pedal pushers (slacks that came slightly below the knee), knit turtlenecks, and pendant necklaces. I think hers were green and mine were blue. Another time I got some low-cut saddle shoes with tiny black buckles on the back of the heels. Some of the other students said you unbuckled them if you were "available" and buckled them if you were going steady. I wasn't sure about that, so I just kept them buckled. I wore those shoes until they fell apart.

Just the arrival of the latest catalogs at our house in Madras was an occasion to write about. In a letter to us in boarding school, my mother said, "The Sears and Wards catalogs came the other day and you should see some of the new styles! ...When you get back we'll make out an order for underwear, etc. I might even send for something for you for Christmas. What would you like...?" Oh, the possibilities!

After a few years overseas, we came back home to department stores, the first shopping malls, and all things American. We could walk into a store and try on a dress. We could buy shoes that fit and not have to wait months to see if we had made a good choice. But while we were in India, the Sears and Wards catalogs were not only a way to order the necessities, they were our windows to the styles, trends, and fads of our homeland.

DAYLILY FARM

The grass hadn't been cut for weeks, but that didn't seem to bother the fifteen or twenty people wandering the grounds of the old house. A weathered sign among the weeds said it had once been part of Daylily Farm. There were still a few daylilies lining the twisting driveway, but nothing was left of the farm itself except for the large hill surrounding the house.

I was there among the curious that spring day because of an ad I had seen in the newspaper. I had come for the auction.

I parked at the Sears Warehouse across the street and climbed the steep driveway that had been hacked out of the side of the hill when Shady Grove Road was widened. At the top, sitting grandly in the shade of a dozen ancient oaks, was the house. Four sets of double doors opened onto a porch that spanned the front of the ground floor. Four dormers peeked from the slate roof on the third floor, and in between, another long porch on the second floor spoke of genteel early morning break-fasts, wicker chairs, and summer lemonade. Ivy climbed the back walls of the main building and a screened breezeway connected the house to the six-car garage and the living quarters above it. It was easy to imagine a time before automobiles, when the building may have been a stable for horses and carriages.

From the hill I could see for miles, although the view of what had probably been fields of corn and pasture when the house was built was now filled with highways, businesses and congestion.

The auctioneer raised his bullhorn, breaking the stillness. "All bids are for the structure only. Dismantle it or bulldoze it into the cellar, I don't care, but in two weeks, it must be gone, down to ground level. The land belongs to the highway department."

With that, he began chanting, his singsong voice rising and falling in the breeze that ruffled the leaves overhead. I looked down at my shoes, damp from the long grass, wanting to be sure he didn't mistake any movement of mine for a bid. Everyone clustered around him just stood there, too. Nobody bid. Nobody moved.

Finally, the auctioneer dropped his bullhorn to his side. "Is anybody interested in this house? Are we going to have a sale today?" I lowered my eyes to the grass again. "What about for a dollar? Surely there's more to be salvaged from this building than that. It has a slate roof. Look at the copper gutters. Now, come on, people. What am I bid?"

Again there was no response. Had everyone come out of curiosity the way I had? Or was removing such an immense building more than anyone wanted to tackle?

The auctioneer waited in silence, then sighed. He handed out his business cards and headed down the driveway. The small crowd dispersed.

I walked across the porch and into what had been the large living room. Dirt crunched under my feet, echoing on the wooden floors. The walls in the room had been stripped down to the lath where paneling had once been nailed. The unfinished bricks of the fireplace were laid bare —whatever had covered them had been pulled away and removed. An oak banister and stairway still curved past the arched window, but in the kitchen, the stove was missing. A musty smell rose from the darkened cellar steps.

I looked around at what was left of the house. The once-grand old lady was now tired and desolate. Her innermost being had been exposed and people were eyeing her aging parts rather than seeing the noble whole she once had been.

On my way out of the kitchen, something caught my eye. Although the entire house had been stripped of everything that could be removed, on a hook hidden behind the door hung a yellow flowered apron. Like someone devastated by a tornado or a flood who clutches the single photograph or child's toy to help them remember better days and happier times, it was as if the house was holding tight to that apron —a reminder of when the kitchen was filled with the aroma of baking on a snowy day and children played in the warmth that was home. As I left, I gently pushed the door back to where it had been, leaving the apron hanging snug against the wall.

The big white house never did sell, although it remained standing for much longer than two weeks. Word was that vandals were chased out from time to time. Graffiti marked the walls.

Then one night, as I was driving home well after midnight, I saw orange flames leaping high into the darkened sky above the hill. I stopped among the fire trucks and hiked up the driveway. The house was burning—too far gone to save. Firemen stood guard, keeping the fire contained. I watched as the sparking walls fell inward, one at a time. And I was glad. I didn't like the idea of the house decaying and rotting from the inside, one piece at a time, as if attacked by a human cancer. Instead it went out in a blaze of glory befitting its earlier life.

There's no way to know now where the grand white house used to stand. The hill was leveled, the giant oaks cut down, and a 6-lane highway built where it once stood. People needed to get to the new subway station, and they needed the services of the mail processing facility that was built down the street.

Daylily Farm? Most people have never heard of it. But when I look across Shady Grove Road from the Sears warehouse, I can still see the elegant white house sitting on the top of the hill, overlooking its fields and meadows. The grass is cut regularly, and the daylilies still bloom.

In His Second Year

I love the time when he first wakes
From his afternoon nap.
I listen for the pad of his bare feet in the hall.
He stands there, silently gazing at me, yawning
And rubbing his eyes with his fists.

I gather him up,
Still soft and rosy with sleep.
He curls in my lap,
His head against me, his eyes half open,
And together we silently rock.
He is so gentle, so little,
And so very vulnerable.
I hold him and love him selfishly,
For he is my baby again
For these few short minutes.

Then, slowly, his drowsiness dissolves.
He wiggles and squirms to get away
And explore this all-too-exciting world.
I can hold him no longer.
He struggles down and runs laughing from me,
And I return to the kitchen.
But I am content.
For just a fleeting, too-brief moment,
I had captured a butterfly in its flight.

RESOLVED

Age 63 birthday resolutions: I will lose weight. I will exercise until my muscles are firm and my pot belly disappears. I will look like I did back when I weighed 100 lbs soaking wet and ate anything I wanted.

I knew it was possible. I knew it was easy. I'd done it before. Why not again?…

So I joined a gym and went faithfully three days a week.

First came the equipment room. It was filled with well-muscled men and tanned, toned women dressed in miniature Spandex clothing. I heard the clank of metal against metal, but the only piece of equipment I recognized was the treadmill. Cautiously pushing the start button, I began walking. Nothing to it. But after a few days, boredom turned my brain to the consistency of spoiled peaches. I tried reading while walking, but the print in the magazines bounced with every step and I got so dizzy I was afraid I'd go flying off the end and land ungracefully in a sweatpants-and-T-shirt heap against the wall.

Maybe, I decided, classes would be better. Yoga. I became very good at lying on my back on my purple mat, palms up, relaxing. In fact, I was an excellent relaxer. It was all those other poses that made me decide I wasn't yoga material after all. The day I crouched on the floor, looked out from under my leg, and vaguely tried to put my foot somewhere over my shoulder, I knew it was time to move on.

I'd never tried belly dancing. It looked like fun. How hard could it be? I bought a pale blue scarf with hundreds of little coins sewn onto it and tied it around my waist. The metal coins jingled happily as I positioned myself in the second row. The music played. I swayed. And then I watched the teacher's firm hips gyrate in directions my hips would never go. Not in a million years. I tried. The jingling, pale blue scarf I'd been so proud of slid slowly to the floor as I shimmied. It went in the car's trunk with my yoga mat.

Line dancing? I couldn't remember the steps if there were more than four. Cardio? My face turned red and I was left gasping for air.

Did my muscles become firm with all of this effort? They did not. They screamed and cramped if I so much as approached the gym, and revolted by keeping me awake at night.

I didn't lose weight, either. In fact, I gained two pounds. And that's when I saw myself reflected in the window of the No-Longer-Petite Store, over near the mall. Windows don't lie. "No matter what you do, woman," it said, "you'll never look like you did 40 years ago. Get real. Check it out. Hair turning gray. Sensible shoes. Square body. Think you're going to look 20 again? It ain't gonna happen."

And that's when the happy truth hit me like a runaway skateboard. I'm at a different stage in my life now. Oh, I can exercise for my health, but nothing will ever give me back the body of my youth. And if I'm able to diet, I still won't end up looking like a thin and sleek magazine model babe; I'll just be a bony old lady.

Me? An old lady? Hey, that's what I am! The thought was liberating. I smiled. I wanted to dance right there on the sidewalk, and even took a few quick steps.

I was finally free to be me. To do what I wanted. To forget about what people expected. And guess what? I realized I was already a terrific old lady. I had smile crinkles around my eyes. I welcomed any adventure that might come my way. And I was equipped with enough padding to make a comfortable lap for grandchildren to climb into.

Age 63½ un-birthday resolution: I'll be what I am, live in the moment, and enjoy the ride. After all, that's what life's all about!

LIVES OF QUIET DESPERATION

It was almost 11 p.m. when Eugene Sheldon's Jaguar approached the railroad crossing. His was the only car on the back road shortcut. He didn't often come this way, especially at night, but he was on his way home from a late meeting and he was tired.

As he neared the tracks, red warning lights began to flash on a pole ahead of him and a clanging bell broke the early summer silence. Eugene pulled to a stop precisely two feet behind the white line and waited.

He opened his attaché case, straightened the folders neatly, then snapped it shut with a loud click. For the most part, there was little to see around him. Trees rose darkly on both sides of the road, turning alternately black and red as the lights flashed. He looked to the right and didn't see the headlight of the train. Something coming from that direction should have been visible because the tracks were straight there. Eugene knew he wouldn't see anything approaching from the left—the tracks curved around a weed-filled hill on that side.

The wax job on his car hood reflected the blinking red lights. "They should replace that missing crossing gate," he noted vaguely. "Someone could die."

Eugene studied the way the tracks glinted in his headlights. The clashing bell pulsed rhythmically in his brain. How easy it would be to die here, he thought. Just pull the car up onto the rise and stop in the middle of the tracks.

The idea made his heart race uncomfortably. Eugene tried to take a deep breath but his collar was too tight. He loosened his tie and unbuttoned the top button. Thoughts of dying were creeping uninvited into his mind lately. He didn't like it. It scared him. Only the desperate contemplate their own deaths and he wasn't desperate, he assured himself. In fact, he was doing just fine.

Take that afternoon, for instance. He turned and rested his hand on the leather attaché propped on the seat next to him. He'd had that case a long time; bought it the day before he started his job at Rickard and Sons and carried it back and forth to work for thirty years. Thirty years. He'd spent all of that time in the accounting department, keeping records, watching finances, and balancing. Balancing everything. Down to the penny.

Inside a tan folder in the attaché was his performance evaluation from that afternoon. "Conscientious and dependable," the report said. Dependable. Eugene frowned. It was a duplicate of every review he had received on every one of those thirty years. Usually he found comfort in his orderly life, but now the utter sameness of his days washed over him.

In the distance the train whistle blew.

He felt claustrophobic, as if his brown, custom-made suit jacket was too small, and he struggled to take it off. No one at work really gave much thought to him one way or the other. He knew that. He was as much a piece of furniture as the coat rack inside the door. Good old boring Eugene. Never invited to lunch with the salesmen or a game of golf with the executives. The secretaries stood by his desk and gossiped as if he didn't have ears.

He'd spent thirty years driving the same roads, spending the day hunched over his work, eating alone in the cafeteria. Same desk, same office. No one really noticing if he was there. And he had fifteen more years of it until he retired.

"I could die tonight and no one would notice," he thought as the sweet summer odor of honeysuckle drifted through his open window.

The train whistle was closer. He could hear it over the clanging of the warning bells.

What would it be like to be hit by a train? He turned toward the sound. Would the front of the train scoop under the car and turn it over and over as it tried to come to a squealing halt? Or would it toss the car into the bushes like a crumpled cigarette pack as it barreled past? It probably wouldn't hurt after the initial impact. He was sure the human body had a way of compensating for pain. If he were hit, he would probably black out immediately. Then there would be nothing. His tidy, predictable, empty life would simply end, replaced by peaceful slumber —forever.

The whistle was louder. Eugene looked at the lighted dials on the dashboard but had trouble focusing his eyes. The engine was in "park" but still running. He felt his hand slowly tighten around the gearshift and move it into "drive," almost as if it was someone else's hand, not his own. The car shuddered slightly. He felt his foot move from the brake to the gas pedal. The Jaguar rolled forward, gradually making its way up the incline to the tracks. The beam from the car's headlights disappeared into the distance as it bumped slowly to the middle of the wooden crossing. Then his foot, of its own accord, moved back to the brake. The Jaguar gently slowed to a stop.

Eugene stared at the shadows in front of him without seeing them. A strange peacefulness settled over him. The clanging of the warning bell faded from his consciousness and the blinking red lights no longer hurt his eyes. Honeysuckle perfume drifted around him and a slight breeze softly fluttered his hair. He was surrounded by darkness and calm.

Then suddenly the ground shook violently. The blast of the train whistle ricocheted around the bend, torturing his ears and boring into his brain. He turned as the million-watt bulb of the train's headlight bathed him in burning, white light. Blinding him, freezing him in place as it would a deer. His hands flew up in front of his face, his body stiffened and his foot instinctively slammed against the gas pedal.

* * *

At exactly seven minutes to eight the next morning, Eugene Sheldon walked through the doors of Rickard and Sons, just as he had every weekday morning for the past thirty years, and just as he would for the next fifteen.

A moment later he entered his office, took off his jacket and hung it neatly on a padded hanger. Neither the receptionist out front nor the secretary passing his orderly desk noticed that he was there.

TAKING FLIGHT

The phone rang. My twenty-six-year-old daughter, Carolee, was excited. "Mom, I think I'll move to San Diego."

Did she say San Diego? Carolee was already somewhat on her own, but hadn't gone far; she was living in a rented townhouse near us in the Washington, D.C. area.

"San Diego?" I repeated stupidly. "You mean like in California?"

"Yeah. California."

I sat down. She'd never been to San Diego. I'd never been to San Diego. I didn't know anyone who'd ever been to San Diego. I wasn't even quite sure exactly where in California San Diego was.

"I checked my office's website and they have a branch there," she said, her voice getting dreamy. "It looks so pretty in pictures."

I glanced through the kitchen window at the muddy snow that had recently immobilized our area for the third time that winter, shivered, and pulled my sweater tighter.

I'd always wanted my children to be independent, to feel free to follow their dreams. But what had I done? She was going to move as far away as she could without falling into the Pacific Ocean. Was it because she had the self-confidence to try her wings? Or was it something I'd said?

I wanted to lift her back into the nest, or at the very least, tie a very long string onto her so I could pull her back when I needed her.

It wasn't long before my husband and I were loading her suitcases and her cat Maggie into the back seat of our car. Carolee sat with her arm around Maggie's travel cage. She wore a coat and knit hat. She'd caught a cold. She looked so small.

The line was long at the airport. A clerk, who reminded me of a sloth blinking in the sunlight, waited on her. He was deliberate and wouldn't be hurried; she missed her flight. This was pre-9/11, and her bags made the trip without her. Fortunately, they'd also been slow picking up the cat, or Maggie would have gone on without her, too.

I looked over at my daughter, expecting her to be upset. She was, but not like I'd thought she'd be. Instead, she was angry, pacing like a fluffed-up chick.

"Here. Watch Maggie," she said. "I'll be right back." She handed me the cat carrier and marched over to the ticketing supervisor. They had a long, animated discussion. My little girl came back triumphant. They would put her on the next flight, and upgrade her, too.

While we waited in the observation area, I took her picture. Her nose was still red from blowing it. Maggie meowed pitifully, echoing the way I felt.

But as I waited and studied Carolee so that I would remember everything about her, she began to morph, like Alice in Wonderland. She got younger and younger, while the cat carrier on the table next to her grew bigger and bigger. No, she wasn't old enough to go off on her own, especially to a place where she didn't know anyone. She was just a little kid. Aside from a family trip to Chicago and one to Houston, she'd never been farther west than West Virginia.

Too soon the airline personnel took the cat and called Carolee's flight. We walked her to the gate.

"Be careful. Don't talk to strangers," I said, attempting a smile.

"Mom, you worry too much. I'll be fine."

She grinned and gave her father and me a hug. Was she being brave? Was it all bravado? We hugged her back and waved as she disappeared through the door and down the ramp to her plane.

Then the whole gate area blurred. I reached for a Kleenex and headed for the ladies' room where I threw cold water on my eyes.

As we drove away from the airport, I pictured her sitting in the plane. She wasn't grown. She was about eight years old and the airplane seat threatened to swallow her. Her feet didn't reach the floor. And while I knew logically that the cat was in the hold, I imagined Maggie huddled under my daughter's seat, meowing sadly.

They had six hours of flying ahead of them. I hoped they weren't too miserable. I needed to reach out and reassure them, but I couldn't. They were getting farther and farther away.

Carolee called when she got to San Diego.

"How was your flight?" I asked, remembering the sad picture of her I'd been carrying in my head since she'd left.

My daughter laughed. "It was great!" she said, enthusiastically. "I had hot towels and I ate smoked salmon! Did you know they have real silverware and dishes in first class? And they give you magazines to read? It was very elegant—the best flight I ever went on!"

I had to smile, partly at her excitement and partly at my racing, mother's imagination.

I guess when a child leaves home, your point of view depends a great deal on which side of the nest you're perched.

Judy Opdycke

FENDING OFF WOLVES

Post Traumatic Stress Disorder, PTSD—labels from my medical files—failed attempts to define the man I have become, or perhaps always was. Doctors question me, but don't understand how three women haunt my dreams. The first is one who may yet destroy me; the second is one who believes me salvageable; the last is one whose life I nearly destroyed. Each in her own way lurks in the shadows like a hungry wolf ready to devour all that I am.

Tania, my wife, the only person who keeps me tethered to this small blue speck in space, still believes in me. But she now insists I leave on a quest to find closure, perhaps peace, which is something foreign to me.

"Even if I go there will be no answers," I insist.

"Then learn to live with the questions." Tania ends the endless discussion, threatening a greater finality. I must make this journey or risk losing what we have.

I go.

After driving many miles, I end up in San Bernardino. This scrappy rat terrier of a town is not my favorite place in Southern California. Located in a once serene valley, it hasn't aged well. On the hillsides, neglected orange groves contrast with Indian casinos and small mansions. Below, the older part of the city sprawls along the valley floor in smoggy disrepair, a graffiti-infested vestige of what once was.

I drive south on Arrowhead Avenue toward the seediest town

areas; bile rises in my throat. Gray shadowy memories skulk through my mind. The wolves are always close by, ready to tear away chunks of sanity if I'm not on guard. Given a choice I would be almost anywhere else.

Instead I come to seek Vivian. Sometimes in my sleep I cry out for her; other times I thrash about cursing her. Two and a half tours of duty in Iraq, where I watched my buddies die, didn't soften my memories of her.

Even Tania, belly swollen with our child, couldn't fill the void that Vivian left in my life. Tania, who sent me on this journey out of love, not anger.

Through the windows of my old Civic I watch the desolate lean against lampposts, bundles of blankets at their feet. Weariness and defeat is written in their posture, on their faces. These I understand, even sympathize with.

It is the visibly young and angry who swagger along sidewalks, wearing baggy jeans and blood dripping tattoos, who jaywalk into the road just to revel in their power to stop traffic, the ones who would pull this country down, never fight to save it, that I find useless. I force my foot to the brake, but wish I had the courage to stomp my boot into the throttle, thereby solving one small problem for society.

Reluctance doesn't keep me from my destination. The Moonshine Lounge appears to my left. I make a u-turn and park in front. The building needs boards replaced, weeds pulled, fresh paint applied. The sidewalk has the rumpled appearance of a slept-in dress shirt. The bar door stands open; loud music and muted laughter drift out.

I pull my six-foot-two frame from the Honda. The injuries that sent me home from Iraq and ended any hope of a military career still slow my movements. I stretch each limb, stalling.

Inside, the smoky darkness hinders my vision, reminds me of my last patrol. Overcome with apprehension I move into the shadows, arms up as if holding an M4. Fear of what may hide in the darkness saps the moisture from my mouth as I begin to shake uncontrollably.

"Need something, fella?"

Startled, I crouch, swing toward the unexpected voice.

A beefy man, whose harsh features fit the environment, studies me.

"Vivian. I'm looking for Vivian." I pause, and then ask, "She still work here?"

"Yeah." He studies me, tilts his head toward the far end of the bar where a worn-out blond is serving drinks. "Little old for ya', ain't she?" He chuckles, casts a knowing look. "Gimme your name. I'll tell her you're lookin' for her."

"No, I'll wait."

He shrugs and leaves me on my own.

A time-fogged mirror covers the wall behind the scarred bar. My image stares back at me through world-weary eyes as I select a seat. Instinct says I'm in dangerous territory, asking to be wounded.

I vaguely remember Vivian's scent, and recall her touch—sometimes gentle, sometimes clawed. But I have no memory of her face and no photo to help me.

"Hey fella. Hear you asked for me," she says. "What'll it be?"

Vivian reeks of booze and tobacco—different than what I recall. I look into a face that has aged in much the same way as the town.

A double scotch, that's what I want. But I order a draft beer, then I lean back to watch her.

She leaves, but quickly returns bringing a frosted glass brimming with foam. "You new around here?"

"Been here before. Long time ago."

"Marine, huh?" As she asks the question, her fingers stroke the emblem tattooed on my right bicep. No recognition on her face. Nothing. She seems devoid of emotion; even her attempt at conversation is stilted, automatic—a feigned interest.

It's only small talk—nothing that matters.

"Remember me?" I ask at last.

Her eyes search my face, momentarily curious. Then her expression clouds; she becomes suspicious.

Taking my left hand in both of hers, Vivian, my mother, turns my palm upward, exposing my wrist. There she finds the imprint of the hot iron she pressed against my arm in retaliation for an accidentally broken lamp long ago. She rubs her thumb over the scar, quiet, thought-ful, maybe guilty, before she shoves my arm away and steps back.

"Wait," I say. "One question. Why? Why didn't you care?" There is a lost-child plea in my voice that makes me ashamed.

She stops, studies me. "Not care?" Anger distorts her face. "I got you out, didn't I?" She's pale, breathing hard, "Leave! Now. Noth-ing's going to change. Go!" She turns and walks to the other end of the bar to join the two men who were there when I came in. She doesn't look back.

A familiar nightmare holds me in place. Wolves circle.

I was six years old with the burn still fresh on my arm when the County sent Child Protective Services to our filthy apartment..

"Take him. He's nothing but trouble," Vivian told them. She watched without emotion as I was dragged away screaming

My next twelve years became a collage of foster homes. There I lived up to Vivian's words. I was often a problem for those who tried to help. Always I held the futile hope that she would come for me.

A second image, one that often follows the first, bursts into my mind.

I, who always followed orders, searched for insurgents in a nameless village. Entering one small house ahead of the others, rifle ready, I heard movement in the corner of a room. Just before I fired I made out the woman kneeling on the floor; she shielded two small children, protecting them with her own body. My orders were to shoot anything that moved. I ignored that command. I backed out before other members of my squad could rush in.

"Clear," I shouted. "It's empty."

This is one lie I've never regretted, though in my nightmares the possible outcomes, the 'what ifs', still haunt me.

I pull myself together, push back from the bar and toss a few dollars next to my untouched draft. I'm finished here.

I'm going home to Tania—Tania and the unborn child we will

both protect with our very lives.

I won't let Tania down again. This time, I promise myself, I will do things right; I will look forward, not back. My head lifts, my shoulders straighten.

Once more the wolves slink back into the forest—waiting.

FIELD TRIP

The phone rings, jarring me awake. I stare into the slobbery mouth of Mischief, my Shih Tzu mix, who begins to alternately lick my face and dig at my pillow in search of a misplaced Milk Bone.

I shove the pup away and grab the phone. Canyon High School has a sub job for me—my first. I punch the right keys to indicate acceptance, replay the tape with the regular teacher's instructions, take notes, and hang up. How hard can a biology class field trip to the city zoo be, even with the bad-rep students from Canyon High?

To get to this point, I survived the dubious experience of student-teaching biology classes to the privileged at a pricey private school, while I dodged my Dad's advice to become a research scientist. I push thoughts of my father's disapproval away as I hurry out of bed. It's six-thirty Monday morning; there is less than an hour until the class begins.

Field trip means casual—I hope. I rush to pull on jeans, grab my college sweatshirt with USC emblazoned across the chest, shove my feet into jogging shoes, and run a brush through my short blond hair. I toss a banana and a granola bar into my purse. Daisy Arnold, substitute teacher, is ready. Bring it on.

Twenty minutes later I pull my Civic onto campus and slide into one of the few available parking slots. Inside the office, I check the clock. Yes! I raise a fist, triumphant—I'm on time.

The gargoyle planted behind the desk that displays the nameplate Mrs. K. Lawson, Office Manager, mumbles, "Room 49. Last building before the bungalows." She continues with mundane directions and advice. "The aide scheduled to go with you phoned in sick. Bus leaves for the zoo at 8:45 sharp. Be on time." She pushes two keys across the desk. "Room key. Bathroom key. Do not use student bathrooms." With a flip of her fingers, she dismisses me.

"Have a nice day," I say. I smile, hoping for a kind word. She doesn't return the smile. "Good luck, Miss Arnold," she says. She looks grim.

A tiny particle of doubt, uncomfortable as a grain of sand on clean sheets, begins to form in my mind. *I can do this, right?*

In the classroom, I glance at lesson plans, study student worksheets, figure out the computer part of taking attendance, and graze on my fingernails. The bell rings. Students wander, stroll, saunter, or strut into the room. Most of them tower over me. They ignore the seating chart and sit wherever they please. I figured this out because, unless Joshua Contrain switched genders over the weekend, the mini-skirted girl in seat number twenty-one is an imposter.

A kid moves toward me. "Hey, you new here?" he says. He has red braces on his teeth that give the appearance of either final stage gum disease or of a recently fed vampire.

I back away.

"Hey, don't stress. We're friendly. Like, real friendly." He steps forward into my space.

A beefy kid, with the beef in all the right places, moves toward him. "Beat it, Germaine."

Germaine obeys.

Now Macho man moves in. "New student?" he asks me.

"Sub," I reply. I step away from him.

"Uh oh," he says. "My bad."

He turns his attention to the eligible females in the mob who are chanting "Mateo. Mateo."

I draw in a deep breath and nearly drown in the heavy odor of sweaty male, lip-gloss, perfume, tobacco, TicTacs, and hair spray all bonded together by the faint, sickly-sweet scent of pot. My already taxed psyche reaches overload. I'm supposed to be the one in charge

25

here. I snatch a black marker and scrawl Miss Arnold across the top of the pristine whiteboard.

"OMG. That's permanent marker," a feminine voice squeals. I rub a finger across the letters. Definitely permanent. I refuse to panic. I'll deal with eliminating my autograph after school.

I turn to face the students. "Please take your seats," I say.

No reaction.

Since both of my parents worked, my three younger brothers were often left in my care. As a result, when I use my best drill sergeant voice a charging rhino would pause mid-attack to follow my orders.

"Sit. Down. Now."

The gang turns. They stare, fumble toward seats, and fall silent. It doesn't last long, but I manage to finish taking attendance and complete a permission slip count while I ignore the growing restlessness of my charges.

Then Glenda arrives.

A stick of a girl with a dark, tangled mane of hair stands in the doorway flapping a piece of paper at me while emitting sonic screeches —eardrum-shattering sounds that make me cringe. Another girl, who I recall responded to the name Bonita earlier, rushes to greet the newcomer.

"This is Glenda. She's going with us today. She has her permission slip." She shoves Glenda forward and points to the paper. My confusion must show. She lowers her voice. "Special Ed. Doesn't like changes."

No kidding, I think, stunned into silence.

"Don't worry. Glenda's great. I partner with her. We have a buddy system here." Bonita again. She is a frail-looking girl who must weigh even less than Glenda.

When at last we board the bus, Glenda hand-flaps her way to a seat near the front of the bus. No one, not even Bonita, sits with her. I consider objecting, worry that forcing someone to sit next to Glenda might embarrass her, and decide to stay out of it. Once the rowdy mob is more or less settled, I park myself beside her. I'm rewarded with howls and shoves. Her movements become increasingly frantic.

Bonita shouts. "She always sits alone. Likes her space. Move."

I move.

The driver, Chuck, who looks way too old and ill to drive any vehicle on public roads, grips the back of his seat and gives safety instructions in a monotone. Nobody listens, except me and perhaps Glenda. She watches him, her hands suddenly motionless.

Bonita leans across the aisle to provide me with a brief, whispered synopsis of Glenda. "She's really smart. Dad's a mechanic. She works with him. Has since she was little. Can fix anything. Even drives the tow truck on their lot."

I find the thought of this kid driving less than comforting.

Glenda is huddled at the far end of the seat, pressed against the side of the bus. Her knees are drawn up to her chest, her hands flutter, and she emits whistle-shrill shrieks at regular intervals.

The driver does my job, his way. He yells at the kids. "Shut up or I'll stop the bus."

They ignore him.

I tune back into my responsibilities, guilty of losing focus. I'm supposed to be in charge here. I shush the kids; they ignore me.

"Silence." I roar out the command, startling them into one more quiet moment.

Glenda rocks in her seat, humming softly.

Mateo turns around to annoy Glenda. "Not riding the short bus today?"

Bonita, the fragile looking pit bull, attacks. "Shut up, stupid." Mateo backs off. His face tells me he feels successful; Bonita's attention was the goal all along.

The trip takes eons. I want off the bus. The objective of visiting the zoo is for students to learn about one of the ways species have adapted to survive by observing the hierarchy of baboon social behavior in action. A video of the group on the bus would serve the same purpose, I'm thinking, and might save the district a few dollars and a lot of hassle.

A headache blurs my vision by the time we arrive. Good old Chuck, the driver, has made clear his dissatisfaction with my mob control strategies. His consist of frequent threats to the students. As a candy bar wrapper flutters past my head, I comfort myself with the knowledge that Chuck's methods are even less effective.

When we do arrive, I herd students through the group entrance, counting. I come up with a head count slightly over the thirty-one I expect. I try to convince myself that too many is better than not enough. I give up that idea and manage a recount. This time the count is thirty-one.

I pass out assignment sheets along with maps to Baboon Mesa, remind them to meet at the exit gate at precisely one o'clock and wish them gone. Pods of students scatter in every direction except the direct route to the intended destination.

A check of the area near the baboon enclosure seems to be my best next move. Maybe some students will actually show up. I manage two steps toward the start of that mission before Bonita, who tows a reluctant Glenda, steps in front of me. "Hey. Can we hang with you?"

I nod my assent, force a smile, and move on. The two girls tag along.

Surprise. Two groups from my class have actually found their way to the baboon area. The geek group huddles together, seven of them, working on questions, taking careful notes. I leave them to the task.

The loser bunch, who number five, taunts, throws out disgusting jokes about baboon butts, and posture in lewd imitation.

"Knock it off," I say. "Get busy on the assignment."

They turn to toss inappropriate remarks at me.

"Stop." Bonita interferes again. She steps between the losers and me in an attempt to protect me the same way she protects Glenda.

I resent her interference. That resentment flares when she dares to try to explain her peers.

"Some aren't comfortable with their own identities. They go weird when faced with stuff like this." She points toward the baboons.

I remain silent, but perch on a nearby bench to rethink career choices, while I attempt to keep score of how many students actually show up to complete the required observations.

At half-past twelve I meander toward the exit. Bonita and Glenda trot along, sometimes ahead, sometimes behind. They often stop on their own to check out various confined creatures as they go.

I'm content knowing that most students made some attempt to work on the assignment and apparently all stayed within reasonable limits of behavior. I've heard no alarms going off, no announcements of leopards set free, no call for me to report to security—all good news. Now I need to get them safely on the bus. Research sounds better and better—nice quiet lab, an hour for lunch.

By one-fifteen the students are on the bus. I follow and attempt to relax into the seat behind Glenda, who shies away.

Bonita scoots onto the seat next to me. "Driver looks wasted," she says.

I glance up. He looks even older than he did this morning. He's pale. His face glistens with sweat.

I shove past Bonita to approach Chuck. "You okay?"

"If I wasn't, I wouldn't be driving this tank."

I don't push him.

Glenda and Bonita are the only ones who observe the exchange. The others jostle for seats as they toss insults back and forth across the bus.

Fifteen minutes into the trip back to the high school I wish I'd confronted old Chuck. The bus lurches forward on Hilltop Drive and careens downhill, swerving back and forth. Chuck falls to the floor and becomes wedged between the seat and the accelerator. Students scream. I freeze. Glenda shoots into the aisle and climbs over the driver. She takes the wheel in time to keep us on the road.

Mateo is right behind Glenda. He drags the driver out of her way. Two of Mateo's homies hurry to help him.

I watch the scene unfold as if sitting in a theater, popcorn in hand. Within seconds, each one a century in length, the excitement ends. Glenda drives the bus safely into a pullout space and parks it. Mateo performs CPR on the driver. Students grab cell phones from their pockets.

I've already called 911.

Fire trucks, police cars, and an ambulance arrive. I call the school office to assure Mrs. Lawson that the kids are fine, thanks to Glenda.

By the time a fresh bus pulls up, the police are through with their witness interviews. Students board a field trip bus for the third time that day; each one slows down to praise Glenda and slap Mateo on the back. They smile in my direction—boisterous now—immortal once again.

Anxious parents, summoned by their kids' excited cell phone calls, have gathered at the school. Dismissal comes within minutes of our arrival.

When I go to thank Glenda, I make it a point to stand back, respect her space. "Awesome driving," I tell her. She bestows a quick, shy smile on me.

Mateo is harder to approach. We both know he's the reason Chuck will live despite a severe heart attack, but now he's avoiding me, as if he fears I plan to praise him and totally blow his tough-guy image. I stand by the exit and wait. As he passes I call his name. He slows, dares me with his eyes. I reach up my right hand. He relaxes and gives me a high five, neither of us speaking a word.

The day is almost over.

I stay to straighten up the classroom and discover that hand sanitizer will take permanent marker off of a white board. Cleaning done, I leave a brief note, aware the absent teacher will know more about the events of the day than I do long before he reads my message.

A shadow appears in the doorway. Dr. Milan, Principal, has arrived. I wondered when she would show up. There goes any thought of a teaching career, I think.

"I hear this has been quite a day." She smiles.

"Quite," I reply. *Scientific research, here I come.*

"I hesitate to ask you after your little adventure, but would you consider finishing out the week for us? Mr. Winchell is quite ill and expects to be out several days."

When I don't answer, she stumbles on. "He'll fax over lesson plans for the classes each day. Will you take the job?"

No way, lady. Those words sit on the tip of my tongue, unspoken. A single word struggles past them to reach Dr. Milan's ears.

"Yes," I say.

Sorry, Dad.

SOME SMALL GOOD

Sometimes, although I try to never dwell on what cannot be changed, or what might have been, I remember. Once upon a time, as a child of minor royalty, I ran in joyful abandon through the meadows of spring, loved, even a bit spoiled by the servant in charge of my care. Those memories have no place here. But be assured, I did not always crawl in the dust with the lowest of the low.

Among my current companions, I am unique. For while it was not always so for me, those around me know no other existence. They do not understand that they are the fortunate ones.

Now each day, unnoticed by the milling humanity that passes by, I observe. Ever a watcher, I am silent among them. What I see often makes me wonder—if all the evil in the world were wiped out, eliminated, what would be left? Perhaps there would be nothing at all. I no longer believe that the good, which reportedly exists in all of us, is real. So I keep my own counsel and keep my eyes open.

My first awareness of passersby is often the shoes they wear —the fine leather which marks the gentry; the sturdy boots that protect the feet of those fortunate enough to have employment; the worn out, too small, holes-in-the-sole shoes of those living on the brink; and, too often, the calloused blue-from-the-cold bare feet of those who live as I do.

Occasionally my first impression is of enough interest that I look up through my mask of rags to study trouser cuffs, or the hem of a skirt. But most often I study the timbre of the voices, the sounds of the town—the rattle of a carriage, the whinny of a horse, the crack of a whip—all of the cacophony that marks my days. There is little I fail to notice.

Now I catch a glimpse of small leather boots, the color of spring leaves. They are quite finely made. With a startling ring of metal on metal, a coin drops into my cup. I look up through the filthy film of fabric covering my face. Another coin drops. Billowing folds of pale green wool brush against me. I have not touched fabric of such quality in years.

"You are here every day. Do you live nearby?" The voice is sweet, musical. She gestures with delicate hands, as she turns her face to study me. Hazel eyes, the color of her dress, surrounded by a gentle, appealing, not quite pretty face, gaze down. She glows with a certain inner beauty. I know her. And I know how often she journeys down High Street, where she goes, who she meets.

I hold my emotions in check. I must not reveal anything. I rarely speak, and that habit stills my tongue now. My mind bids her leave; instead she stays.

"Why do I feel so drawn to you?" she says. "There are sufficient beggars here that no one should stand out."

I give no indication that her words have reached my ears.

Another woman, visibly a servant, dashes through the mud, dodging horses. Her drab dress accented by her white cap and apron mark her. But her manner is not the humble one her garments imply. I know her, too. I allow my lips, hidden under the gauze mask, to curve in a crooked smile.

"Miss Elizabeth, Mr. Dodd will surely have my hide and my job. I've lost track of you again. Come away. Leave this poor soul to its day's begging."

I watch the plump, once-familiar figure of the older woman, see her pause, consider.

She knows. I shake my head to quiet her.

She returns the slightest nod.

Did she bring the girl here for her own purpose? This is

the woman I once teased about being my fairy godmother as she protected me from my father's frequent wrath. *Could she mean me harm?*

The young woman says, "Emma dear, don't scold. I was causing no mischief." She turns to obey. But she looks back over her shoulder, as she is hurried away. "I will see you soon," she mouths to me.

Three days pass and Elizabeth stands before me again. Angry at my own folly, I have watched for her. Glad, yet disappointed, when she doesn't return. Now she is back, and I once more wish her gone. She does not know—cannot begin to understand—what sadness she brings with her. As before, she drops coins into my tin cup. I, forever caught between the charity and the indifference of others, do not want aid from her.

"Winter is coming. Do you have a place to sleep out of the cold?" she asks.

I think of my snug little cocoon of straw and rags beneath the supports of the West Bridge. Yes, I have a place to go, and this winter, when the worst weather comes and the wind blows across the river, I expect to die under that stone buttress. I do not mind, for I am content there.

Now, though, for the first time in months I wish to speak, long to warn her of what I have seen. The sound of my voice passes my lips as a croak. "Beware", I say.

"Did you say 'Beware'?" Her eyes have widened. I see fear in her eyes. The reputation I once gained as a seer must have reached her ears.

"Your betrothed. Beware. Twelve, Castle Road." The sounds I make can hardly be acknowledged as human, and certainly not as my once pleasant voice, but I can be understood.

She is gone. I long to call back the words—words I know will cause her pain—for she has been kind to me. Perhaps there is some small good left after all, but now I have frightened it away.

Two weeks have passed and Miss Dodd has not returned. Most of another week passes. And then a coin drops into my cup.

"Do you perchance still read?" The servant woman has returned. So, she does know me.

The woman holds out a folded paper, sealed with wax. I remember that she cannot read or write. I reach out and accept the paper, suddenly aware of the thick broken nails on my soiled, calloused hands. How I must reek of the horse manure, slops, and spittle I am forced to crawl through each day.

"What you told the girl has served to anger Mr. Dodd, something fierce. But you've saved young Miss Dodd from a most unfortunate marriage. Thank you." She curtseys before she turns and disappears into the crowd.

I wait until dusk. I am alone then, creeping along on my way to my nest under the bridge. I stop before the last light fails, and pull the letter from beneath the raveled bit of rope that serves me as a belt. It is a gracious thank you letter. Nothing more.

Soon the frequent rains of summer have turned to the constant drizzle of fall. Fog and cold are now a part of each day. The cough that has plagued my damaged lungs worsens.

The next time I see Elizabeth Dodd the fine wool of her garments is a rich brown with the reddish cast that is called russet. I sense even before I look upward who stands before me. Once again she drops coins into my cup.

"How did you know?" When I do not respond she continues. "I do believe you have saved my life. I saw him strike her. What if I had married this man? A vicious man, who would hit his mistress, the mother of his children, is bad enough, but the children were there to see. How dreadful their life must be. My servant woman accompanied me. She has spoken to my brother on my behalf. I am certain Edward will see to Mr. Goodman's ruin. I fear it is the woman and the little ones who will suffer most, though."

I remain mute, which serves to encourage her to fill the silence. She asks me to be her friend. What a strange alliance this would be. And what would her brother make of it? Once I knew him, too, and I have little desire to renew the acquaintance.

35

"Your heart does not appear broken," I manage to say.

To my surprise, she smiles. "No, I could scarcely abide him. But he was reportedly of wealth, and dear Edward could not refuse when he asked for my hand in marriage."

Ah, yes, dear Edward, I think.

"There is a shed at the back of our home," the girl says. "It is quite snug. I asked the man who keeps the garden to clean it out and repair it. Would you consider? I mean… Oh dear, I hope I'm not being too forward, but would you consider living there? The little room can be heated. And Edward has given permission, just for the winter. I've secured a cot and a chair. Cook has promised scraps from the kitchen."

"You know nothing of me," I say. I suspect, that like most who approach me, she does not even know my gender.

"I know only a little, true," Elizabeth replies. "No one seems to know much about you. But I know you spoke up to help me. Now I hope to be of help to you. The shed is yours if you wish. You saved me from a wretched existence, and you've protected Edward from certain humiliation on my behalf."

She leaves me torn between what I have grown to believe about mankind, and what I was once taught. How dare she show me kindness in the midst of a hateful world? Confused and angry, I do not answer.

But fate takes a hand. I am ill when she next sees me—too ill to deny her wish. She sends a cart to fetch me. There is a doctor waiting when I arrive at my new home. More a tiny house than a shed, I think, as I gaze in wonder at its sturdy walls crafted of stone. But I have little time or energy for contemplation. I am hurried into my new abode, for the doctor's time is precious.

I discover the doctor cares nothing for modesty. He pulls my ragged clothes free of my feeble grip. I hear him gasp. "You were terribly burned, miss. However did you survive?"

I do not reply to his question, do not tell him about my fall backward from a tree in the garden. I wasn't supposed to climb. Girls of good breeding were discouraged from such activities, especially fourteen-year-old young ladies.

A housemaid was heating water for the laundry. I fell from a branch into the fire, tipping the scalding water across my face. My legs, back, chest and jaw were deeply burned. My hands and lower arms remained unscathed.

I lived two weeks in agony. Doctors declared nothing could be done. I heard them tell my father I would die. "If only there were some way her misery should be stopped. Keep her quiet. Use laudanum generously. Pneumonia will take her soon and that will be a blessing."

But I did not die.

In agony as muscles constricted and what had once been pale, smooth skin turned to gnarled scars, even as infection took a toll, I lived on. I did not wish it so, nor did my father. He needed me to make a good marriage. Now I was useless.

I, however, share none of this with the physician. Nor do I tell him what followed. I have never told the story of the night my father wrapped me in a blanket and took me away from my family —away from all I had ever known. He, assisted by another who remained silent, took me to the abbey and left me on the steps outside the gates.

The steam, which engulfed me when I was burned, had left me without a voice. He had no fear I would tell my tale. It was months before I could do more than croak as if I were a toad in the garden. I have improved, but never regained my original voice.

Still, my father put his face next to what was left of mine. "Say nothing. Write nothing. This is for your own good. You will be safe here."

"Papa, no." I heard my brother's voice then. "You can't do this." My older brother was pleading for me. Yet he had helped carry me.

The sound of a hand slapping flesh made my ruined body flinch. "You will say nothing—ever. Katherine died in the night. Do you hear me? She has no future with us. Here perhaps she can find some small purpose." My parent's noble speech was punctuated by another slap. Mute, I listened as the carriage moved away. I had been abandoned—left alone in the darkness.

Someone else found me before the abbey gate opened in the morning. That is a story I still cannot revisit, even in my own mind. If I thought I had found Hell before, I soon learned I was wrong. And still I survived.

I was abandoned again, left in the forest, closer to death than when I was left on the abbey steps. This time the gypsies found me. Their care was gentle and effective. I began to thrive despite my wishes. Be assured they had their own purpose. For the next four years I begged on the street, earning money only for my benefactors. In return, I was fed and cared for.

I never found the courage to leave them. I learned the art of telling fortunes, developing a mystique only enhanced by the covering I wore over my face and the hoarseness of my voice. Thus, I earned additional money for my caregivers.

One bright summer morning, soon after they had deposited me on the street with my tin cup, the sheriff drove the gypsies away from the edge of town. At the end of that day, no one came for me. I never saw the tinkers again.

But I share nothing of this with the doctor.

The physician finally allows me to cover my body and my face. "Your vision was saved. How fortunate you are." A strange statement, I think, to label me fortunate.

He continues. "Your lungs sound as if they are clearing. Hot tea, warm broth, will help. And rest."

"She will stay here. We will take care of her." The familiar melodic voice states this in a manner that brooks no argument.

And I do stay. Loose, warm garments are fashioned for me. Discarded hats and bonnets are wrapped with new veils to conceal my scars. There are soft undergarments and wool stockings. And elaborate shoes and boots, too shabby for my benefactor's taste.

I have not worn shoes for years. To my surprise I am able to slide my damaged feet into the soft leather. I believe it is all too good to be true. I am not wrong.

I am content, happy even, in my quiet shed. It is warm and comfortable. Each morning Edward's gentle wife, Margaret, comes to inquire as to my welfare and brings with her a tray bearing thick warm porridge, rich with dried fruit and cream.

The kitchen maid brings me food noon and evening, none of which appears to be the kitchen scraps promised. She brings hearty thick soup, served with soft white bread for my midday meal. I am quite certain that every evening I share the same fare those invited into the dining room partake of.

I learn from Margaret that Edward is out of town on business. I fear all this will end when he returns.

One evening, after I have lived in the little room more than a month, Edward Dodd knocks at the door that I have come to think of as mine. When I bid him enter, he strides into the warmth of the room, bringing with him a sudden chill.

He slows and looks around, nervous. "You will think me mad, I'm certain, but I must ask a question. My sister, Elizabeth, tells me you go by the name Cat. And the physician tells me you are badly scarred. I must know, is your given name by chance Katherine?"

So, he is at last beginning to put the puzzle together. I have been called only "Cat" for years, but I have never forgotten who I once was. I am strangely sad with the knowledge that I will lose my little home, but, as always, I speak honestly. "Yes, I am Katherine."

He is on his knees before me. "I thought you were dead. After father died, I went to the abbey to inquire and they knew naught of you, or so they claimed."

"They spoke the truth, as I do. Others took me away before the gates opened."

"Can you ever forgive me for the wrong done to you?" He is grasping my hands tightly in his. *Are those tears on his lashes?*

"What can I do to make things right, to make amends? Anything. If it is within my means, I will grant your every wish."

I do not reply for long minutes. "Edward, I will forgive you, of course. You were only a little older than I. But if you ask me to forget, I shall be forced to refuse."

He bows his head. "I do understand. I fear you are more generous than I would be." He at last reaches out to pull me forward and hold me tightly against his chest. He releases me to ask again, "Please, let me give you what I can. Just ask."

"I would ask to be allowed to live out my life right here where I am, in this lovely little room. Shh." I put my finger to his lips. "Do not object so soon. This is all I require. Also, you must never reveal my identity to Elizabeth. I prefer her to believe me a new friend, rather than a sister she has no memory of. Also, I would ask that you allow her to marry for love, not money."

I stop, unused to prolonged speech. Edward fills a cup from the pitcher the servants keep filled with clear water. I drink deeply.

At last I speak. "I have one more request. It will be far more difficult to grant than the other wishes. Of course you also must convince your wife that this is a wise decision. Bring me paper and pen and I will direct you. Then you and Margaret must decide." I know Edward's wife to be a kind, gentle person or I would not dare to ask this of my brother.

I am immediately granted my first wish. A solicitor is summoned to draw up a legal document, granting me the right to live out my life in the tiny space I call my own.

I then share with Edward my observations regarding a mutual attraction between Elizabeth and one David Chauncey—a man of good, if modest family. And I present him with the promised note, which I have written in my unpracticed hand.

***

It is spring now. Elizabeth is betrothed, with Edward's blessing. David will be an excellent match for her, I know.

Today as she comes to tell me her plans for a summer wedding, I have ventured out on a wagon the gardener made for me. It allows me to propel myself without dragging my legs in the dust. I have planted bulbs along the path; they are now budding.

I am busy listening to Elizabeth prattle while I pull weeds from the soil, when Emma, the servant of my childhood, Emma who raised Elizabeth after our mother died at her birth, Emma the only person other than Edward to know my story, comes down the pathway. At her side skips a small girl, the beloved adopted only child of Edward and Margaret.

"Auntie Cat, Auntie Cat, look at my new dress," Angelique calls to me as she runs ahead of Emma, who has helped to make such moments possible. I reach out my arms to hold the child tightly against me. My beautiful daughter, a child conceived in the violence of the hours that followed my abduction from the steps of the abbey, is safe and loved.

The only time I ever understood my father, even if for only a brief moment, was the day I returned to the steps of the abbey to leave my baby. But I did not abandon her there. I left her in the arms of the nun who opened the gates that morning.

Now as I gaze upon the child, my hardened heart begins to soften and unfold, much as the buds on the daffodils are readying themselves to bloom. There is indeed some small good in this world. I now have everything I require to make this life worth living.

Marlys Collom

Card Room Dealer

On lower 4th Avenue
between the Balboa Theatre
showing 24 hours of porn
and the tattoo parlor,
sat a card room, Cirrottos.
In this land, prior to its
transformation from red light
district to Gaslamp district,
a place foreign to me, was my new job–
though I didn't know the language
or have a GPS to guide me.

His name was Coffee, his skin
the color of coffee and cream.
On his head a fedora with a peacock
feather tucked into the hatband.
His voice, just above a whisper, inquired,
"Hey Mama, wanna join my stable?"
I, horse crazy and naïve, mistook his intent.

He was the first of the pimps I met.
Frisbee drove a pink Cadillac. Big John
was cruel; his girls had bruises which
they tried to cover with makeup—in vain.
He made them beg for drug money,
for their dreamland of reprieve.

Vice Squad, drug dealers, johns, regulars,
played cards here. Eyes wary, ever vigilant,
there were rules, there was a code of conduct.

One night, on break, I stepped outside and
over a drunk passed out on the sidewalk.
I tried to help him up so he wouldn't be arrested.
Coffee called me inside.
"Don't do that!"
"Why?"
"If he wakes up he'll think you're gonna roll him."

Coffee taught me to walk close to the curb,
away from doorways with snatching hands.
When blood spattered the plate glass window
during territorial fights, I was not to look up
from the table. I was not to palm chips or
give the wrong impressions. This was a place of
sordid clear truth, required for survival.

One night two beautiful women entered,
dressed as hookers, but without the
worn down, worn out, defeated look.
They were organizing a union
called Coyote for prostitutes.
They mistook me for a "sister."

Driving home late one night, away from
sirens blaring, red lights of cruisers
reflected from streaked windows
of human despair and discontent–
I decided to find work uptown,
among the wealthy, the privileged.

And I did, still on 4th Avenue, years later.
From card room dealer to corporate Vice President,
though the former wasn't on my resume.

This new environment had crooks too,
they were disguised in Armani suits.
I learned the ropes, was paid well.
Granted perks—a company car,
spa membership, valet service.
A corner office in Mr. A's building.

I once again had to learn the lingo.
Thought we were talking about
Tahoe when offered cocaine by a
Mr. San Diego who asked if I skied.

I liked the ambience of this new world.
The stakes were higher, the pay better.
But I missed the raw honesty of the other.

Hookers were here too,
they were called trophy wives;
their husbands, well-healed pimps,
peddled investments.

A San Diego Charger

He was playful, a childlike giant.
We shared M & M's during class
and conjured ways to humble our
egotistical, arrogant Mensa teacher
in a school of adult students, at
a career-expanding boot-camp.

One day we met for dinner at Trophy's.
I hadn't known he was a celebrity Jock
until they announced his presence and
comp'ed the meal. He laughed at my naiveté,
liked that I wasn't dazzled by his stardom.

Another time, at lunch at the Imperial House,
seated in their high wing-backed chairs,
devices of illusion, of discretion, of anonymity,
heads swiveled and peered unsmiling at us.
At first I thought they recognized him,
until he placed his dark, manicured hand
on my white arm and said "Leave it alone"
in a gentle warning voice. Fame wasn't drawing
the attention from these men in penguin suits,
color was—fearful color, a darkness
perceived as tainting their colorless world.

We drove down Imperial Avenue one day,
he signed autographs at stop-lights. Another
free lunch, soul food piled high on plates the
size of platters, in a Mom 'n Pop restaurant,
a mere mile from my childhood home.

My friendship, without strings or guile,
was like a pair of comfortable slippers
for him. Women usually chased or tempted,
or sought attention from his presence.
But like childhood friends, we talked of
hopes and dreams and of secrets that are
still kept.

My Passion

My passion is a thousand pounds of powerful,
sweating, rippling muscles between my thighs.
My body conforms to his body,
he senses my intent through my movements.
We are a two member herd, this horse and I,
our joining the realization of a long-ago dream.

Only one of us can be the leader.
I am required to prove myself worthy
in order to gain rank and trust from him.
He demands strength of body and character
from me, and certainty and confidence.

He is an ancient breed, instinctual.
I am a student learning the language of "Horse".
Soon his nature will become my nature. He will
learn to sense my hand and body signals.

II.

Before us is a poppy and lupine strewn valley.
The breeze-stirred hills of prairie grass undulate,
laced with lavender-and-cream shooting stars.
The meadowlarks sing the song of our joy, as
hoof-beats pound the open plain in gaited rhythm.

Ahead is a riverbed. Coarse, multicolored sand
marks the entrance to the waterfall and the pool
where my horse, like a sham moose, will wallow
and roll in delight. He left well-groomed,
but will return home with his shining chestnut
coat camouflaged in dripping moss and trampled
watercress.

This day of sun and sky and open spaces
will become a memory with feeling-tones,
a newly composed song.
I am addicted to this rapport,
we are two beings who understand each other.

III.

My husband and I ride on a cattle round-up in Anza.
The cowboy's face is the color and texture of my saddle.
He wears a sneer partially disguised by a faint smile
as he eyeballs our sleek, elegant Tennessee Walkers–
wearing custom-made saddles and quarter-cropped manes.
He is astride a sturdy, stout-legged bay Quarter horse,
specially bred for range and ranching.

Our horses, Tigger and Midnight, think this is a fun new
game. They are curious and eager for this new adventure,
their ears are perked skyward, their bodies on full alert.
Adrenaline-pumped heartbeats pound through the saddles.
We all learn the rules together and are amazed by the
speed and agility of the rangy steers who head for cover
in the prickly, overgrown scrub.

Our horses pursue the wily and half-wild horned beasts.
They leap off edges of water-worn ravines, nostrils flared.
We urge them on, ride as though we were adolescents,
at one with their county-fair fun-zone ride movements.

After eight hours of pounding his saddle with his
troubled mile-weary ass, the cowboy comments
that he will never see these as "sissy" horses again.
For they have rocked us gently with their plantation gait
across the ranch land of gopher-holed ground,
rugged rocky outcrops and sun baked hard pan–
unspooked by a rattlesnake on the trail.

As daylight wanes, the cowboys are homeward
bound in their rusted stock trailers. Still immersed
in this new adventure, my lifetime husband,
our horses and I stand atop a small rounded hill,
a foursome facing west to view gold and pink tinged
UFO shaped clouds.

My horse's nose is buried in my hair.
Midnight rests her massive head on my
husband's shoulder as he tenderly holds my hand–
we are one with each other and with the world.

The Bay of Fundy

Fishing Trawlers, white as the foam whipped from
wind-blasted waves, with names of wives or daughters
imprinted on their bows. Their trim painted cobalt blue
or rust red, their wheelhouses with submarine windows
meant to deter the sea, float at anchor in a small bay lined
with colorful shanties.

Strewn about are piles of encrusted lobster traps and
ocher coiled rope. Nearby, yellow rain slickers are
draped over well-used wooden saw horses. Dried salt
has formed in the seams as sea-water evaporated.
Here and there, a fisherman with calloused hands makes
repairs to boat or gear—an unending cycle in a difficult
life lived for love of the untamed sea.

Fishing poles with oversized reels that cost thousands
of dollars, electronic depth finders and GPS systems are
lashed in place with bungee cords—at the ready. They
are unlocked and unguarded and catch cod from a
depleted Atlantic Ocean. The fish are so full of mercury
they are sold only to China or Japan.

~ ~ ~

Driving inland, we pick Macintosh apples from laden trees,
buy apple cider fermented at the local mill and watch
Canada geese through a restaurant window that juts out
over a marsh and pond in this small Nova Scotia village.
The smell of baking Irish soda bread almost distracts me
from the lobster lunch I relish. I wonder if the lobster is
as full of mercury as the cod.

~ ~ ~

Now the tide is out, so far out we drive across the exposed sea-bed to an island once inhabited by a minister and his family; their homestead self-sufficient. Curious free-range cattle and sheep approach. We share our juicy, just-picked apples. From behind the weathered barn with a sagging roof a llama emerges. He rejects our offering, but accepts a caress as he blinks his warm, brown long-lashed eyes and surveys his kingdom with the sometime-moat.

The fishing trawlers lie at angles on the seabed bared by retreating tides. Some of the ships are supported by steadying structures that were unseen beneath the water when we visited this dock earlier in the day. The bay is emptied of water. It has left behind a rich smorgasbord of food for long-billed birds scavenging among tufts of sea-grass and beached, barnacle-hulled boats.

The cycle of life is more apparent in this land—the elements seem elemental. I drown in sleep each night, immersed in the sound and smell of the saltwater. My dreams of living here are revised over breakfast the next morning at a small café the fishermen frequent. I overhear their talk of preparations for another long, harsh winter soon to descend, and of how brutal the biting black flies and swarms of mosquitoes were a few months ago.

Chelsea

Love is a Labrador
the color of late summer wheat.
Ghirardelli-dark-chocolate eyes
peer over her shoulder
from a bent cage at the pound.

She has dignity, this girl, yet
cowers in fear from past abuse.
We ignore the signs of submission,
praise the strength that lurks within
and soon her being is filled
with trust and constant joy.

Her first day at the lake, we discover
this water breed doesn't know
how to swim. She sinks three times,
frantically thrashing. The next time
we borrow our daughter's wise Shepherd
and all swim together. Chelsea,
exultant, has discovered her passion.

Prowling coyotes meet their match.
They make the first move, then
she throws them to the ground,
as a wrestler would to the mat.
Places her paw on their chest,
victorious, but not boastful–
when they submit, they are
released to resume their hunt.

New collar and leash, both
the color of ripe tomato,
secure her to a silver post
in front of an antique store.
Inside, shelves with glass treasures.
At the back of the store, we glance up.
Proudly prancing, the escape artist
approaches, tail wagging in wide sweeps.

Her ecstasy is leading her pack,
a man, a woman, and two horses,
along mountain trails and lakes,
past trees whose trunks serve as woodpecker
storage, drilled holes filled with golden acorns.

Mouth smiling, body bounding through tall,
coarse grass along the Pacific Crest Trail.
Startled, Chelsea leaps and catches a
slow-to-launch meadowlark.
Shocked surprise registers on her face.

She is only frightened of fireworks
and guns; shivers and hides
when they invade her domain.
The vet's X-rays reveal birdshot
scattered throughout her body,
along with a more insidious invader–
cancer—everywhere.

We add new memories to the old.
Lift her into and out of the van.
At work she sleeps, curled at my feet.
At home, two other cancer patients,
my husband and horse—both on chemo,
fight their own battles. Only one wins.

In our front acreage is Chelsea's new bed,
a freshly dug pit,
lined with lime and rose petals.
My horse survives another year.
My husband lives still.

Southern California Snow

Michigan family tells me of bleak
gray winter days, of damp earth,
sodden from too much rain. Of
soil erosion and gooey mud and
of their sunlight-deprived depression.

They watch and wait for falling
temperatures, anticipate ice fishing
after the first dusting of snow that is
likely to come in the form of a blizzard
which will freeze the lakes.

Here in Valley Center, in this first week of
January which has delivered an unexpected
dusting of ice crystals, my husband awakens
me at five in the morning, his face alive with
childhood memories of playing in the snow.

With flashlights we explore the wonder of
blossoming roses—crimson, amber, salmon,
all dusted with crystalized snow. Palm trees,
wild lilac, our cars and our neighbor's solar panels
all glisten white in our beams of light. Snowflakes
briefly drift lightly onto our hair and shoulders.

As the sky lightens in dawn's glow, the scope of
this rare occasion reveals itself as far as we can see.
Mt. Palomar rises majestically in deep angora
brilliance, coated from the uppermost peak to
the groves of avocado trees on the valley floor.

Change, unexpected change; pristine, pure,
untouched, fleeting. Clouds disperse in the new
morning sun, diamonds reflect from snow crystals.
Brittle spider webs become pliable once more.

The morning news predicts it will be in the 80's
next week.

Playboy Club, San Diego
1982

At the newly opened Playboy Club in Mission Valley,
I, the only woman in a group of penguin-suited men,
wore my cream wool rich-bitch suit as I wined and
dined prospective investors, and pitched a real estate
opportunity.

The bunnies hugged and complimented me,
taught me the sideways dip used to serve drinks.
Their costumes were thick with metal stays
which served as a built-in corset. The bras were
super padded to thrust breasts upward in gravity
defying rounds and to serve as armor against
touchy-feelies from men's wandering hands.

Rosie, the club manager, gave me a backroom tour.
Shared dressing rooms, posted rules, required
congeniality. The girls told tales of past gigs in
stripper bars off Midway Drive. The Playboy Club
paid more, hooking was forbidden, pimps barred.
They all aspired to work at The Mansion.

The girls were treated with an upscale respect here,
unlike at the pink stucco-walled, garish all-nude
dancer club in Point Loma where I was once
asked to dance for a couple of hundred and tips.

The Survivors

Over mismatched coffee cups, the men with
calloused hands and weathered faces speak in
survival mode, telling their life stories.

John, born in Estonia, was sent by boxcar when
he was twelve to a concentration camp.
He is the only survivor from his family and village.
He was one of the prisoners who chewed on the
leather of the shoes of the dead to quell the
hunger pangs that were constant from forced labor
at the death camp.

Paul, his skin the blue-black of pure African, tells
of growing up in the deep South, where, as a little
boy, people hated him, but he never knew why.
Didn't comprehend until years later that a millimeter
of skin-color could render you non-human.

My husband, one of a family of eleven, lived in a
one-room, unfinished basement that flooded when it
rained or when the snow melted. When he was seven
and hungry most nights, food was what the children
hunted, or trapped or stole from fields.
His mother, destitute and full of despair, had given up.
His father was dead, killed in a war in a country
that is now a tourist destination. The children were
sent to an orphanage, a place of practiced cruelty.

These men don't indulge in self-pity or compare their
tales with one-upmanship. They speak simply, in a
matter-of-fact tone—that only magnifies their sufferings
to me, the listener nearby.

Transmutation

Dedicated to my horse, Tigger, and the Wolf Sanctuary in Julian, CA

In a land of turbulent unborn lava,
pulsating within its deep caldrons are
boiling mud pots and geysers that erupt
in power displays skyward. A threat is hidden.
It deceives by the regularity of timing.

Yellowstone, named Mi tse a-da-zi,
Yellow Rock River, by the native people,
is now home to a relocated grey wolf.
He is learning the lay of the land, staking
out territory, discovering food sources.

From the top of a mountain he surveys
the forest and meadows through his amber,
lupine eyes. Glowing, they appear backlit by
the warm mid-afternoon sun.

It is summer now, the time of bounty and surplus.
From his vantage point on a boulder overlook
he senses dusk, the time of the hunt.
Perhaps tonight he will also meet his mate.

In severe winter months, neighboring ranches
will tempt with herds of sheep and cattle,
and shaggy winter-coated alpaca and horses.
Deep within his cells is a memory,
triggered by the musky scent of a horse.

A memory of inheritance of life as a cub lived
on a wolf sanctuary in Julian where survival
was nurtured in him with the flesh of a horse.
A horse well loved by a woman who chose to
transform the dying body of her beloved, his
source of life transmuted into another living being.

The now feral wolf howls as the moon rises,
a howl robust with life and freedom.
His mournful call reverberates, echoes through
miles of mountain passes, sends waves of tones
to a ranch where a woman is awakened,
unsure whether she has heard a wolf howl
or the neigh of a horse.

Freedom Realized

China

Roaming a dusty lane of centuries-old, hard-packed Asian soil,
I explore the village compounds on the outermost edges
of Beijing. Peopled by venerated elders clad in Mao pajamas;
one woman with bound feet smiles a warm, toothless smile.
She grasps two home-made wooden canes, struggles on her
lotus blossom feet, an imposed beauty meant to imprison her.

Tai Chi practitioners in local parks futilely guard the old ways.
The clamor of modernity pushes against them. High-rises in the
distance crowd, threaten their homes, their communal lifestyle.
The packed mud-floored wood homes, swept daily, encircle a
shared cooking fire. Elder women beckon me to warm by the fire.
Bicycles lean against outer walls, next to a tethered donkey.

I, an obvious foreigner, am now lost and in need of a toilet.
Ahead is my needed refuge. A mud-walled, doorless shed
announces itself by odor. Inside, briefly alone, I straddle
the recessed trough dug the length of the dirt floor. Soon
neighbors curious about me enter this one-room-for-all.
Fortuitously my long wool skirt affords some modesty.

Still wandering later in the day, an old woman, her creased
face a testament to her life experiences, approaches me and
speaking through her fluent daughter asks:
"What is it like to have more than one child?"
Never faced with birth restrictions in my country
the impact of this question stuns me.

Israel

The Kibbutz, alongside the blue-green sea of Galilee,
is bordered with thriving vegetable gardens
planted in rich black dirt that had to be
flooded multiple times to leach salt from the soil.
This well-tended land appears peaceful, a safe refuge.

Ahead the children's school playground, empty
but inviting, has swings, shining metal slides,
a multicolored jungle gym in the center.
Closer now, I see the bomb shelter bunkers
a few feet from the play equipment.
The school's plaster walls are degraded, pock-marked
from bullets. I count 89, but there are many more.

U.S.S.R.

This vast grey country of Russia, with crumbling concrete
buildings on the verge of collapse, has signs imprinted with
names of places I have read about or seen in movies—Gorky Park,
the Kremlin, St. Basil's. My son and I explore. He, with a
U.S. Secret Clearance, who speaks the native tongue that enables
us to navigate our way, unhampered by government assigned escorts.

The subway stations serve as art galleries, with high-arched ceilings
inlaid with tile mosaics in primary colors, depicting brave workers
and muscular women, portrayed with their arms raised in defiant
revolution.
There is no graffiti in sight, no street people, no panhandlers.

Riding the subway, windows reveal that female construction workers
are in the majority in this population of war-reduced males. Ancient
construction equipment seems to diminish the Communist threat.
We lack the knack for departing a subway train. Bodies packed
like Russian nesting dolls hamper our exit, we miss three stops.
Smiles appear on too close faces, a kind soldier clears a path for us.

Old women, like the scarves they wear, are called "Babushkas".
They sweep the sidewalks and streets with straw brooms.
Departing a museum, I smile at one of them, thank her in Russian.
A smile transforms her dour face—she approaches me and buttons
my jacket, rearranges my scarf, then escorts us to the door.

Everyone stands in long lines for hours each day to make
purchases from near-empty shelves in state-run stores.
This deteriorating city reflects its deteriorating government.
Tourists are herded to Barioshkas, shops meant to impress,
open only to foreign visitors. I purchase feminine products for
my new Russian friends, one of many items not available to them.

While I'm taking a bath in tea-colored water in our overheated
hotel room, my son in the next room discovers a listening device
in his bedside table. We leave it and restrict our future conversations.
I, a foolish, naïve, arrogant woman scoffed at the State Department
briefing—it seemed so contrived at the time.

The next day, on the way to the Bolshoi Theatre a man approaches,
his arms crossed, a scowl etched on his face, he attempts to menace.
Affronted and rebellious, I boldly mirror his glare back at him.
Lift my chin in defiance as those around us lower their heads,
avert their eyes—they know the rules of this game.
My son gently squeezes my arm in warning, until I practice
submission to this purposeful intimidation.

United States of America

On a mountain ridge I sit poolside in our cabana at home.
Lounge in a chaise with flowers and fern Hawaiian print
cushions while sipping hot, peach tea. Fog has settled into
the valley this early morning hour. Hilltops in the
distance appear to be islands. Dew beads sparkle on
an orb weaver spider web, anchored to King Palm trees.

On the table at my side are three-ring-binder photo albums.
One for each journey is stacked, one rests open on my lap.
Photographs intended to evoke memories, feelings,
revelations, and experiences accomplish their purpose.
Turning pages, I recall being jet lagged when I returned home.

I remember feeling overwhelmed as I entered our supermarket.
Row upon row of abundantly stocked shelves displayed fresh
produce, unspoiled meat. Available, whether needed or just wanted.
As I transferred heavy bags of groceries from the metal cart into my
car I thought of a man in China who proudly bragged to me of his
wealth because he had two bicycles.

I have just returned from the journey through Russia,
with its deprived, frightened citizens, restricted and full of want.
Assigned housing, assigned jobs, encouraged betrayals. They
were frightened of freedom, an unknown, derided state of being.

I think about the Sinai Desert where a black-robed Bedouin woman
in a remote village answered a question I asked. One an interpreter,
a hitchhiking ex-military "desert rat" we had picked up on the roadside on our unscheduled foray, at first refused to ask for me. Her
dark, expressive eyes, crinkled at the corners, revealed her
veil-hidden-smile. I knew there would be no offense.

My husband and I watch the news on T.V. "I was there, right there!" I sing out, memories flooding. Now, when reading a passage in a book, or watching a movie, there is clarity because a woman or man or a child in a far-away place shared their life, their feelings, their views.

Grandmother

She lost her hat,
her glasses,
her purse,
and her mind
long before I met her.

Grandpa called her "Muvver"
I called her Grandma,
but she didn't call me anything
because she couldn't remember
who I was or who I had been.

Our bond was playing cards.
She was happy then, smiling
with glee when she drew
a red one to place on her
upturned red ones—
        Black on black
        Red on red.
There were no other rules
to our game.

Till my mother came over
to the card table and tried to
patiently remind Grandmother
the *correc*t way to play rummy.
Then Grandma would flee
the table crying.

That's another thing we shared,
crying in frustration
over inexplicable rules.

Anza Borrego Mud Caves

A red-tailed hawk circled overhead
as we entered the narrow slit opening
in a mountain of dried mud that reminds
me of the sandcastles we made as children
by dripping wet sand, one blob at a time,
until a mound formed giving an appearance
of melted candle wax.

The twisting cave has been carved by
torrents of water that roared down
mountain passes when rare rainstorms
passed through these desolate Carrizo
Badlands.
Curiosity lures our family onward.
Grandparents, children, grandchildren.

The walls of the cave crumble when touched,
a fine powdery dust that was held in place by
a thin crust of dried mud. On the uneven floor,
at the base of the slanted curve of the wall,
the silt is still damp where shallow pools formed.
In narrowing places we slither snake-like
across patterns of mud-whorls.
Though millions of years in the making
these formations seem fragile, vulnerable.

It is cool in the cave. We are thirty minutes into
the exploration. We wonder about the extent of
the lack of natural light so we briefly turn off our
flashlights—the darkness is complete, as is the silence.
I try not to think about flash floods or earthquakes
while we are deep inside this sculpted fissure of earth.

Columns and spires, rises and falls, cubbyholes
and forks in the trail challenge sure footing.
As the batteries in our small flashlights began
to dim, we reluctantly turn around and laugh
as we finish the last ten minutes without light.

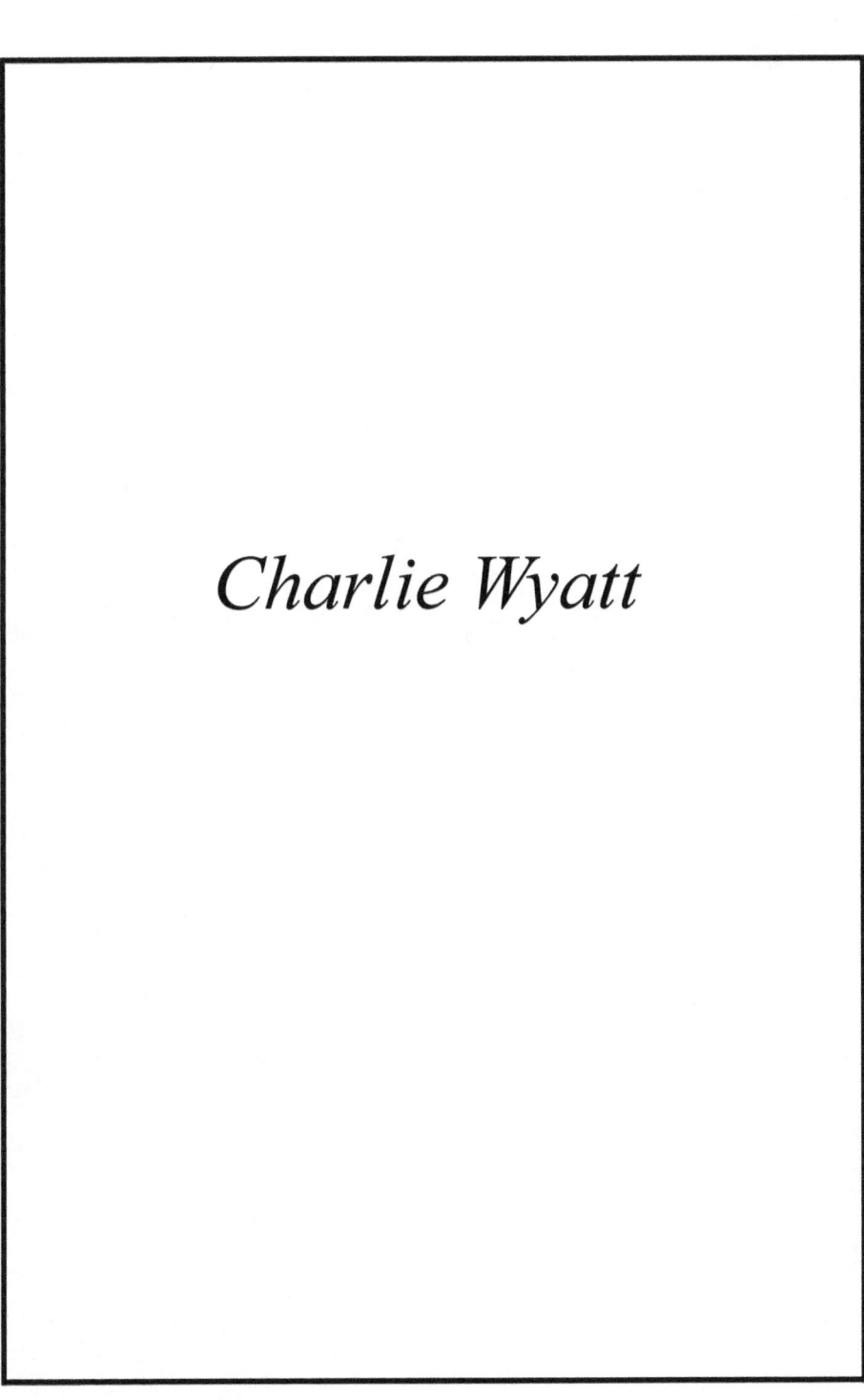

Charlie Wyatt

DOWN BY THE RIVER SIDE

The normal placid tenor of life in Toadvine, Alabama—a village on the banks of the Warrior River—was disturbed, and the residents were discussing the person responsible.

Zeke Hargrove was back home, staying at his mom's place on Kitty Branch, his four-year Army tour complete. His dad had died two years earlier and it was unclear what Zeke's plans were. Word was, if he signed up again, he would receive a $12,000 re-enlistment bonus. He had done okay in school and more than okay in the Army, so rumor had him moving to Atlanta and enrolling in Georgia Tech.

Tom Greenstein, a professor at the local junior college, remarked to his wife that Edna Mae Collins wouldn't like hearing that. "She's been sweet on him ever since he was in the seventh grade and she was in the fifth."

His wife said, "Well, she'll have some competition, you can bet. Zeke Hargrove always was a nice boy—polite and good-looking. He's just got more handsome and grown up since he's been away."

Zeke himself seemed unsure of his future. His friend, Ben Jenkins, was home on leave from the Air Force. Zeke told him, "I don't know, Ben. I don't want to go back into the Army. I've had all I want of the heat and dust—and being scared and jumpy most of the time. If I re-upped, it would be back to the Mid-east for me, that's for sure. Sometimes when I was over there, I'd think about this big river, the cool evenings, and how good it felt on a summer day to jump in. I'd think about our old crowd and football nights, or just sitting around shooting the bull. Before I joined up, I was hot to get away, see places, do things. I guess I didn't realize that old Toadvine wasn't so bad."

Ben said, "Well, don't re-up, then. You're what? Twenty-two?"

"Twenty-three next month."

"That's what I'm sayin'. You've got no real responsibilities, you can do whatever you want to. How 'bout school? Maybe go to college."

"Yeah, I been thinkin' along that line. I've got the G.I. Bill, plus I've saved up a good bit. No place to spend it over there. I might like to be a civil engineer—build things, you know, instead of blowing 'em up. Georgia Tech has a great engineering school. Only thing is Atlanta's a big city. I'm not sure I'm cut out for a city dweller. All my life, before the Army I was right here and it still feels kinda' like I might belong here."

Ben smiled at his friend. "I can't decide for you. A man's got to go with his beliefs. Right now, I believe I'll have a beer. You want one?"

"Of course. See, that's another thing. I'm not sure anybody in Atlanta likes me well enough to fetch beers for me."

***

A few nights later at Shooter's Lounge, Zeke was the center of a group of admiring locals. The guys wouldn't let him pay for anything, buying his beer and plying him with questions about his combat experiences in the Mid-east.

Zeke managed to duck most of the drink offers, and say little or nothing about the experiences. About the third time he said, "Nothing special."

Bobby Joe Hester complained, "Whadda' ya mean, nothing special? You were Special Forces, right? I bet you blew up all kinds of stuff, shot up villages, probably killed a slew of rag heads."

Zeke gave him a hard, direct stare. "Here's what I've come to believe. All fighting and killing is bad. War's the worst kind of bad because you don't have anything personal against the people you're trying to kill and they're trying to kill you, just on account of the uniform you're wearing. All this is happening because some old guys, thousands of miles away from the actual bloodshed, have screwed up."

There was a short, shocked silence.

Then Bobby Joe protested, "That's not what you were saying when you first joined up. You were all gung-ho then."

"Yeah, and I was eighteen and almost as dumb as we all were back then, but I'm almost twenty-three and a lot smarter, I hope."

Normally those would be fighting words, but now Zeke had the air of somebody you really didn't want to mess with.

After another embarrassed pause, Zeke said, "I'm afraid I'm not very good company tonight, guys. Thanks for the beer." He left, nodding in passing to some of the other patrons.

After he was gone, Bobby Joe said, "Man, Zeke sure was wound up tight. He used to be such an easy-going guy."

Earl, the elder statesman of the group, said, "Give him a little time. He's only been back a week."

This met with general approval, particularly since Earl himself had returned from Vietnam years before, and had shown a similar distaste for talking about it. One of the unwritten rules in Toadvine was: If it's not your business and it ain't hurting you, leave it alone.

***

The following Sunday Zeke accompanied his mother to the same little Baptist church he had attended as a child. Both before and after the service, a number of families came up to him, shook his hand, and welcomed him back. Prominent among them was the Collins family.

Miss Edna Mae Collins hung back a little, blushing as he took her hand. Zeke smiled at her and asked, "So, what have you been up to, Curly Top?"

She managed to stammer out, "Nothing much."

She felt her heart thump when he said, "We'll have to see what we can do to change that."

After church, Zeke asked Earl to drive his mom back to her place; he wanted a word with the pastor. When everyone else had left,

Zeke helped Brother Paul straighten up the folding chairs.

Then for almost an hour, the two men could be seen walking back and forth past the neatly tended graveyard and down the road to the old ferry landing.

The pastor said, "Is it that you feel you want to stay here, or that it's your duty to?"

Zeke tried to sum up. "I guess my problem is, I really want to get some more education. Over there, life was day-to-day, you know. Didn't pay to think too much about the rest of your life. Mainly you're concentratin' on staying alive and in one piece. Now, since I'm gonna' have to get a job for the rest of my life, I'd like it to be something worthwhile."

The minister, who had known Zeke since he was a small child, asked, "And how does that present a problem?"

"Well, if I go to Georgia Tech, I'll be over there for most of the next four or five years, plus probably away working during the summers. I'd kinda' like to stay here. My mom's health's not the best and I'm afraid it's not going to get any better." He turned, looked out over the river, then said, "This is where I was raised, you know, I'm not sure I want to totally uproot, leave all the people I've known, but I need to decide fairly soon. I have some money saved, but if I don't take advantage of the G. I. Bill, I'll have to take some sort of job."

The pastor asked, "Is that the only college you could attend for what you want? My impression is that the first two years of college are more or less general, with credits that could probably transfer. Have you talked to Tom Greenstein? He's probably the best suited to advise you on that."

Zeke looked up. "Maybe I'll do that. Thanks for letting me bounce these things off you."

The pastor smiled. "You said you wanted a job you liked doing, something worthwhile. That's how I think of my job. Anyhow, speaking purely selfishly, I hope you'll find a way to stay around. No community ever has too many good men."

***

A few nights later, Earl ventured out of his house to enjoy the almost full moon and the mild evening. The rising moon turned the river into a broad silver path, while the trees on either bank provided a dark border.

A little way down the bank, he made out a figure seated on a log, looking out over the perfectly still water. Approaching, he saw it was Zeke.

"Mind if I join you?"

Zeke grinned up at him. "I was kinda' hopin' you would."

Both were silent for a while. Then, without preamble, Zeke said, "I've made my mind up. I'm not re-enlisting. I did my time and I'm through with all that."

Earl said, "Pretty big decision. Not only passing on all that money, but it ain't so easy, making the change from the strict rules and regs of Army life to the mostly live-by-your-own-rules in civilian life."

Zeke countered, "You did it, after Vietnam."

"Yeah, but that was then, this is now, and that was me and this is you."

Zeke didn't reply.

Earl said, "So, what's the plan? Move to Atlanta and go to Georgia Tech?"

Zeke said, "No, I'm staying here. I'll live at my mom's for now. It's just a short commute to Jefferson State. I talked to Professor Greenstein, and he said I can do my first two years there then transfer to the University of Alabama and get my engineering degree. After that, they say I shouldn't have any problem hiring on with Alabama Power or maybe with the county."

Earl said, "You don't think you'll miss travel to different places, meeting different people, maybe doing more exciting stuff?"

Zeke smiled, still looking out over the glass-smooth water. "Nope. As they say, been there, done that. Far as places go, you and I have both seen a lot of different ones. You going to sit there and tell me any of 'em could beat this?" He swept his arm in an arc, taking in the moonlit scene.

Earl grinned, "Yep. When I first got out, I had a screwy idea I'd like to be an illustrator, maybe a commercial artist. I went up to New York City to art school. I'd been to the Big Apple once before, when I was a kid and I loved it then. Took a year for me to figure out I never would be any good as an artist. Friend wrote me George Bishop was selling this place, cheap, and I lit out for home. I spent the four-hour trip trying to make that plane fly faster. Haven't been north of Huntsville since."

Zeke said, "As far as meeting exciting people goes, I guess I'll just have to make do with you clowns around here. I've been doing a lot of thinking. Sure, folks here aren't perfect, but take 'em all in all, they're no worse than you'd find anywhere and better'n most, I think. I guess what I'm trying to say is, this is as close to what people call home as I'm likely to find."

Earl acknowledged that, then said, "So you think you can make the transition from Special Forces Warrior to Warrior River Nothing Special?"

Zeke paused before saying in a serious voice, "Yeah. It was something I had to do at that time, but tonight I was rememberin' one of the old spirituals we used to sing in Sunday School."

He cleared his throat and began. Earl listened to the first line, then joined in. The two veterans of wars separated by half a world and thirty years blended tenor and baritone: "Gonna' lay down my sword and shield, down by the river side, down by the river side, down by the river side. Gonna' lay down my sword and shield, down by the river side. Ain't gonna' study war no more."

SO THEN I SAID TO JOHN WAYNE...

The year was 1964, and for one of the few times in my 24-year-old life, heretofore lived in a take-it-as-it-comes-I-can-handle-anything way, I was extremely nervous. I had been pacing back and forth on the quarterdeck of my ship for thirty minutes, getting more edgy all the time. We were getting underway in twenty minutes and the most important passenger of all still wasn't aboard.

I gave a momentary thought to what the consequences would be if we did sail without him, but quickly realized that was not going to happen. The United States Navy might run a tight ship and sailing schedules were sacrosanct, but there was no way we would sail off and leave John Wayne standing on the dock.

The whole thing started four months before, when I was ordered to report to the captain's cabin on the double. Now for this to happen to a junior officer—in fact the greenest ensign on board—was usually a very bad thing. I made my way there, mentally examining my conscience for what I could have done so bad as to warrant this dire summons.

Once inside, I tried to control my voice better than I could my quaking knees. "Ensign Wyatt, reporting as ordered sir."

The captain, seated behind his massive oak desk, looked me over, much as a housewife might examine a not-very-promising piece of merchandise on a markdown sale table.

"Stand at ease, Mr. Wyatt. You've been with us for how long now?"

"Just over four months, sir."

"And one of your duties is Public Information Officer?

"Yes sir"

I refrained from telling him that that particularly burdensome and thankless job was invariably foisted off on the newest junior officer to report, as soon as the previous assignee could swing it, a fact which I'm sure the captain was well aware of anyway. He sat stroking his chin and looking alternately out the porthole at San Diego Bay and back at me.

Finally he said, "Read many books?"

I was frantically trying to decide if this was a trick question, designed to trap me into an admission of guilt. However, having learned to read before I was four and done so voraciously ever since, I felt I couldn't deny it completely.

"Yes, sir, when I can," thus hoping to indicate that I would never neglect my Navy duties for mere reading.

He said, "Ever hear of one called..." he looked down at a piece of paper on his desk, *In Harm's Way?"*

"Yes, sir, I have read that one."

He smiled for the first time. "Good. Good. Some bigwig in Hollywood wants to make a movie out of it. Seems this ship is the only one still around that will fit the one in the book. The movie types have apparently convinced Commander Pacific Fleet to let them film on board, as long as it doesn't interfere too much with our normal operations. For the time being, you will be the liaison with Naval Public Affairs up in L.A. Inform your department head that whatever time you need off to travel there and whatnot, you're to have. Keep me informed of any potential problems. That's all, carry on."

Actually I had not only read, but enjoyed the book by James Basset, a World War II action novel set mainly aboard a heavy cruiser very much like our ship, the U.S.S. Saint Paul. Since ours was the only such ship remaining in service, that was undoubtedly the reason it had been chosen.

The next few months went by in an ever increasing whirl of activity for me. With the speed of light—or at least sound—the news somehow spread throughout the ship's gossip grapevine.

By the next day, reliable rumor had it that a) the ship would be going to Australia for filming "because the seasons are opposite there," b) it was being taken out of service completely and turned over to Paramount Pictures, or c) it was sailing the next week and staying at sea for two straight years "because the Navy didn't want them commie pinko bastards from Hollywood using their ship."

The lieutenant junior grade who had dumped the Public Information Officer duty on me approached and first hinted around, then demanded his old job back. I had the pleasure of telling him "tough toenails," or words to that effect.

I did, in fact, make several expeditions up to Los Angeles to confer and co-ordinate with Public Affairs in the person of Chief Petty Officer Joe Kuherich. The chief, complete with custom-tailored uniforms and Polaroid shades, had the best job in the entire United States Navy and played it to the hilt. He enjoyed dropping names of his contacts at the various studios and taking me to the "in" places in Tinsel Town for power lunches and nodding to celebrities. But that's another story, maybe even a full length novel.

The upshot of all this was an agreement that the filming on the ship would take place in August. We would be in Seattle for their annual Sea Fair celebration, and the actors and film crew would board there. We would then take a leisurely ten-day cruise to Hawaii, where a good portion of the movie was to be shot. It turns out the so-called Hollywood bigwig the captain mentioned earlier was Otto Preminger, director of such mega hits as *The Man With the Golden Arm, Porgy and Bess,* and *Exodus.*

The big news, however, was that the main character, Captain Rock Torrey, was to be played by none other than John Wayne. Even the real captain of our ship was impressed enough by that to order me to be Mr. Wayne's personal gofer. He didn't put it that way, of course, but it was clear that I would have none of my regular watches or duties during the ten-day trip.

One memorable day, we were invaded by an advance team of film people. There were guys taking still photographs of every imaginable location, other guys with steel tape measures recording dimensions and writing on clipboards. The one in charge, an assistant director I gathered, walked around sneering at everything and making cryptic comments. He was wearing lime green slacks, a white polo golf shirt and tasseled loafers. He even wore a beret, the only person I had seen do that since Edna Mae Thompson wore one the first year in high school, and she was generally considered to be pretty weird herself.

The crowning moment came when he was frowning over the supposed cramped quarters on the ship's bridge, destined to be the scene of much of the action in the film. He was throwing disparaging remarks over his shoulder to his assistant, Megan, who solemnly wrote down every word on her clipboard. She had straight brown hair, harlequin glasses, and a miniskirt, which she really shouldn't have been wearing with her legs.

On a ship, vertical walls are called bulkheads and after backing into the rear one on the bridge for the third time, he turned to me. "This wall will have to come out. There's simply not enough room in this shoebox to get a proper establishing shot or pan around effectively. We'll pay to have it replaced, of course."

I glanced at the two enlisted men standing nearby who were having a tough time keeping straight faces, then explained to the guy that since the "wall" was one-and-a-half inch tempered steel and had been triple welded in place since 1944 when the ship was launched, I doubted it could be removed. He gave me one last dirty look, turned to Megan and snapped, "Studio construction of whatever they call this place."

"Ship's bridge," I told her helpfully.

A few more communications flew back and forth before the ship left for Seattle. There the other actors and film crew began filtering on board but with departure time set for 9:30 a.m. sharp, there was still no John Wayne.

Nine-twenty found me sweating—in both senses—at the end of the gangplank, fearing a crisis of monumental proportions.

Then, like the cavalry officer he had so often played who always showed up in the nick of time to save the day, John Wayne arrived. A car traveling considerably too fast for safety on the crowded pier screeched

84

to a halt, and a large figure, unmistakable even at a distance, emerged. He reached back in and hauled out the largest suitcase I'd ever seen.

He yelled, "Thanks, Bill" at the driver and started for the gangplank. I sent a sailor down to take the bag for him, but the big man waved him off and came striding up in that distinctive way he had.

I stepped forward, stopping two paces from him and said, "Welcome aboard, Mr. Wayne. I'm Ensign Wyatt. I've been assigned as your personal liaison for the trip. If you'll follow me, I'll show you to your stateroom."

He followed me down one deck and a few feet along the passageway to the cabin of the ship's navigator, who had been temporarily forced to double up with the operations officer.

When he had plopped the suitcase on the bunk and shed the sport coat he had been wearing, I asked, "Is there anything I can do for you at the present?"

"Waal," he said, in the drawl that sounded phony when anybody tried to imitate it, but somehow seemed right for him, "if you could scare up some aspirin, I'd be grateful. I got a head like seven Swedes."

I hurriedly went back to my own junior officer bunkroom, grabbed the bottle I knew one of my roommates always had on hand, and handed it over in less than a minute after hearing the request. He shook about six into his palm, tossed them down without benefit of any liquid, and heaved a sigh of relief. He gave me that smile that you seldom saw but when you did, it was like a the sun breaking through clouds.

"I think we're going to get along fine. What did you say your name was?"

"Ensign Wyatt, Mr. Wayne."

"Well, hell, I can't go around calling you Mr. Wyatt all the time. Your mother must have given you at least one other name."

I gulped, but said, "Usually I'm called Charlie, Mr. Wayne."

He stuck out one very large paw. "Good enough, Charlie, and for God's sake drop the Mr. Wayne. I'm Duke, named after my dog when I was a kid, if you can believe that."

"Certainly Mr. Wayne, I mean Duke. Is there anything else?"

"Do you play chess or bridge?"

"Yes, sir. I mean, I play at them. I'm probably not very good at either one."

That was sort of false modesty. I had supplemented my very meager funds in college by winning at bridge rather regularly at a penny a point. As for chess, I hadn't had much opportunity to play opponents with any pretensions to being expert, but I figured I could hold my own against a 58-year-old guy who had been too busy making almost two hundred movies to study the game seriously.

He said, "Good, after lunch we might have a game or two. Right now, all I want to do is grab some shut eye and give the aspirin a chance to work."

I went to find my roommate and explain that I would replace his aspirin as soon as I had the chance. He was thrilled to think the great John Wayne was treating a hangover with his aspirin, and told me not to worry about replacing it, just get him to autograph the bottle before he left the ship.

Lunch was something else, let me tell you. The executive officer sat at the head of the table as usual. On his right was Otto Preminger, on the left John Wayne. I had the seat next to him, the only naval officer at the table under the rank of full commander.

Working down from there on either side were Kirk Douglas, Carroll O'Connor (not particularly famous then, but immensely so later on with "All in the Family" and "Heat of the Night"), Burgess Meredith (a fading former leading man, later most famous for playing the Penguin in the Batman TV series), Tom Tryon (who Preminger had tried to make a major star a couple of years before in *The Cardinal,* but who later achieved much greater renown as the author of horror novels like *The Other* and *Harvest Home*). There was even a young Larry Hagman, veteran of a lot of mostly forgettable TV work, who the next year hit it big with first "I Dream of Jeannie" then "Dallas."

Conversation was general, mainly questions from the senior naval officers about the movies, but with some interplay between the actors. Preminger said little or nothing, being on record as stating that as far as he was concerned, actors should speak their lines of dialogue and then shut up. He considered the only difference between them and badly behaving children was size. With his balding head, German accent, and general Prussian manner, he could have easily been cast as the mean Nazi commandant in one of his own movies. The rest seemed ordinary enough, except for their voices, all resonant and pitched to carry to the back of a theater.

After lunch Duke and I did engage in chess. The first game, he came out early with concentrated attacks, me frantically defending, and in the end earning a hard-fought draw. The next, knowing what to expect, I let him over extend and trapped his queen, leading to my checkmating him on about the fifteenth move.

The last game, we both played more cautiously at first, but I got a lucky break when he overlooked a sneaky move I made with my knight and I managed to capture one of his castles. Even then he fought desperately to the last pawn before conceding, a trait I learned over the next few days was an integral part of his makeup. It just wasn't in the man to give up.

I, who had been a fan for as long as I could remember, knew of the rumors that he had had a lung removed the previous fall due to cancer, a result of his previous five-pack-a-day consumption. The studios wouldn't let him announce it publicly until several years later, but in private he made no secret of it. "Yeah, I beat the big C that time. Wasn't quite ready to cash in my chips just yet."

Shooting was scheduled to start early the next day. I managed to get a copy of the script and studied it that night with an intensity I had never given to school subjects.

Early the next morning I got my first experience in the very confusing business of making a movie. The initial shock was that the scenes were to be filmed out of sequence. I know now that this is pretty much standard, enabling the director and film crew to set up at a given location and hopefully get in all the scenes set there before moving on to a different place. The drawback, as I saw it, was that the actors were required to learn bits of totally unconnected dialogue and deliver them with the emotion consistent with the scene being shot.

The actors themselves, however, seemed to have little trouble with this, switching from lighthearted banter to intense drama, minute to minute as required. In addition, a number of scenes were shot and re-shot, apparently so the director could get the angles he could then choose from later and discard the rest on the cutting room floor. Everyone but me seemingly took all this in stride, hardly ever blowing a line or missing their mark, which meant not stepping or standing where they should.

The one exception was Tom Tryon, whose dark handsome looks should have dominated any scene, but who would sometimes blow a line several times before getting it right. Preminger, whose patience was extremely short with anyone else, showed remarkable restraint with him, perhaps because Tyron had been his protégé but also because he had no one else to take the part, since getting another trip on a heavy cruiser was out of the question.

As far as professional skill went, you had to admire both Wayne and Kirk Douglas. The two men were about as far apart in temperament and politics as you can get, Douglas making no secret of his very liberal stance and Duke being an icon for the right. In the movie they were buddies, and on the set you would swear that was true. Off it, they didn't air their differences; they just didn't associate.

Filming usually ran from around eight or nine in the morning until four or so in the afternoon, with an hour-and-a-half lunch break. The evenings were completely free for the movie types and so for me. Movies were shown, but perhaps out of tact and not wanting to favor anyone, none of Douglas', Wayne's or Preminger's.

Duke usually wanted to play bridge. The first time we cut for partners, he and I ended up as opponents. At the end of the evening my partner and I won. He didn't say much, but in future games, he always made sure that he and I were partners.

On a subsequent night, I opened with a rather minimal hand and he responded also minimally, but I jumped to three no trump anyway. I led confidently out, suit after suit, and just delivered the contract on the last card, the deuce of diamonds.

As I gathered in the trick, he said, "My God, partner, you gotta' have the guts of a burglar!"

Coming from him, I took that as a compliment.

"Well," I said, "that was the only way I could see it. No sense fiddling around with it and giving the opponents time to think about it."

He gave that slow nod and said, "Yep, sometimes that's the only way."

The times I remember best are those after dinner when he would just talk. At first some of the other officers would ask questions about the movies and how he got started and what his favorites were and so forth. I suspicion that some of his answers were a little tongue in cheek.

To a question about his personal favorite, he answered *Hatari.* There followed a little silence. Most of us had been expecting a John Ford western or *The Alamo*, the one he bankrolled and starred in, but had lost most of his personal fortune on, when it bombed at the box office.

Someone asked why *Hatari,* an almost B-grade film about animal hunters in Africa.

"Waal," he drawled, "the thing ran way over budget and time, so we got paid for almost five months of riding around in jeeps with no hard lines to learn. It was too damn hot to shoot from about ten o'clock until four, so we sat around drinking and telling lies. My idea of a great time."

Somebody else was rude enough to ask, probably in light of his well-known fondness for an adult beverage or two, if being on a Navy ship without a drop of alcohol to be had might not be a little bit of a hardship.

"Not at all. I like these enforced short periods of being on the wagon. Dries me out and make me appreciate the next tall, cool one."

Later in that week, he and I were talking in his stateroom and a more serious side came out. I remember him saying, "I've tried to follow my father's advice. First, always keep your word. Second, never insult anyone unintentionally. If I insult you, you can be damn sure I intend to."

Another time he said, "I never worry much what people say about me. My family and friends know me well enough. The rest I don't give a damn about."

The ten days went all too quickly as far as I was concerned. We pulled into Pearl Harbor early one hot tropical morning and the film crew started debarking almost at once. Shooting was to begin on the island sequences later that day. They left in little groups, some in vans the movie studio had provided, some in private cars driven by friends there in Hawaii.

I knew from something he said the previous night that he was being met by someone, and for whatever reason, I didn't want any kind of awkward farewell on the quarterdeck with his friend impatiently waiting. However, I couldn't keep myself from going forward to the bow on the main deck and watching for him.

About nine o'clock, I spotted him striding down the gangplank and toward a Cadillac sedan some distance up the pier, as close as the harbormaster would allow vehicles. He was still carrying the big suitcase and sauntering along in that walk that any movie fan could recognize on sight.

When he was just past me, though, and contrary to what I had planned, I called out, "Good luck on the rest of the film, Mr. Wayne."

He stopped short, dropped the case, and looked up.

"What did you call me, Pilgrim?"

I said, "Sorry, Duke. Good luck. I'm sure it will be a great picture."

He nodded and said, "That's better. If they ever let you off of this tub, you oughta look me up at the ranch over in Encino. Anybody over there can show you the way."

I said, "Thanks, I'll do that."

He nodded again, picked up the suitcase and went to the waiting car. I watched it disappear out of sight, then went back below to resume my real-life existence.

I spent the next four years in the Navy and a few more after that in San Diego figuring out what I wanted to do with my life. John Wayne made some more movies including a couple of his best, then the big C attacked again and this time the cancer won.

I never took him up on his casual invitation to visit, and I'm pretty sure he wasn't serious anyhow. But still, over the years that followed, I regretted lots of times that I hadn't at least made the effort. Lots and lots of times.

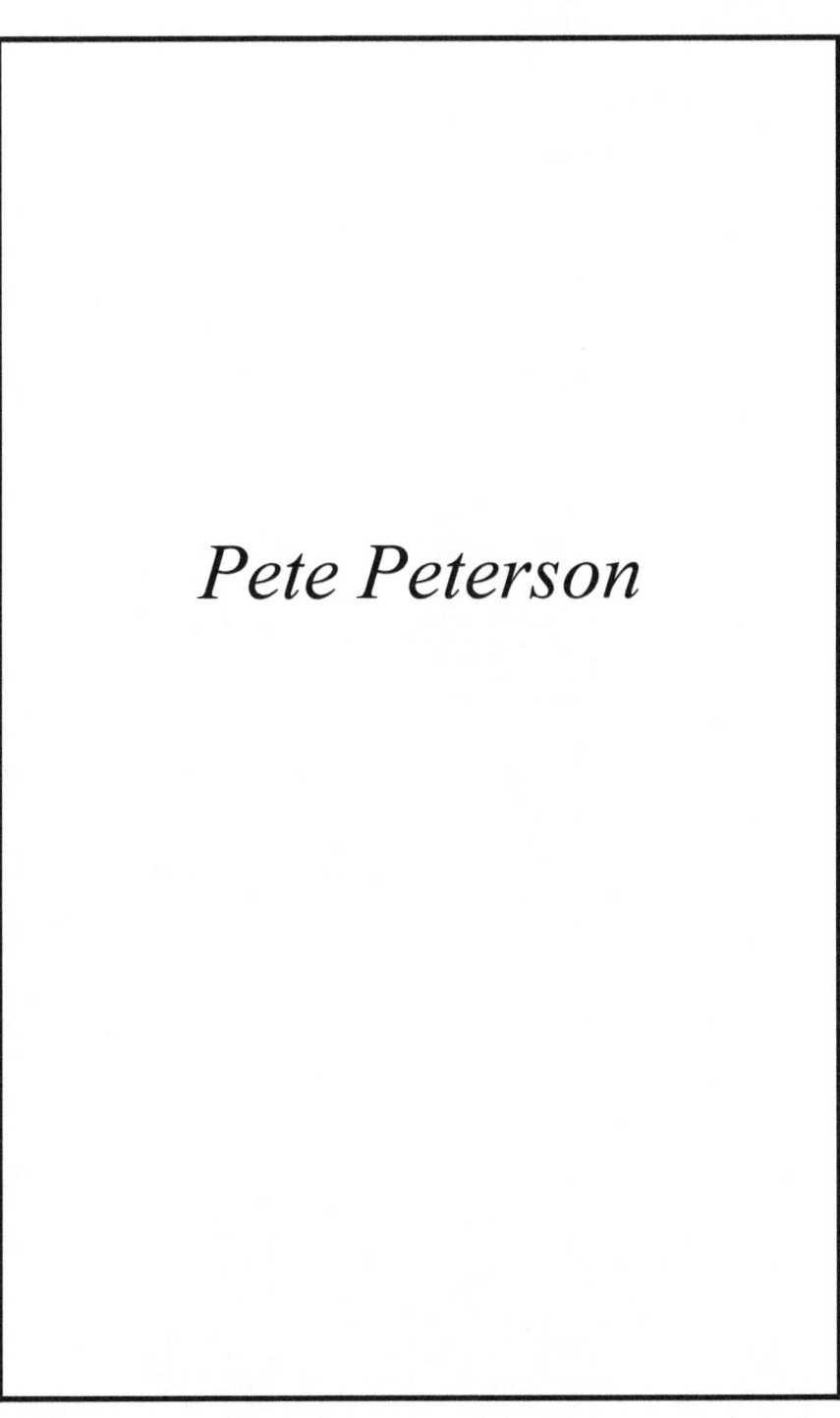

Pete Peterson

WINNER TAKE ALL

It's fight night and my friend Ryman Call is bein' fairthewell clobbered to a bloody mess. Blood drips from his chin, his right eye swole up big as a persimmon. Young Bob Cleary circles Ryman, a hungry wolf after a crippled sheep. Cleary sends a hard left to Ryman's forehead. Ryman staggers like a toddler tryin' to walk. Cleary fires a right to Ryman's belly. Ryman sprawls to the sawdust.

Cleary throws his fists in the air, like he's the new champ. The crowd screams and stomps, glad to see Ryman Call finally gettin' his due, plum happy the local boy they've watched trot off to school holdin' big sister's hand, is doin' the smashin'. They yell for Ryman to get up, they want him beat on more.

I'm Hamas Zanderhook. I cook for Ryman and his three daughters and ride herd on Winder, his eight-year-old boy. I seen all of his slugfests from his first barroom brawl to tonight's donnybrook. This is the onlyist time he's ever ate sawdust. Usually, it's the other feller who's covered with blood and snot, and will mebbe cripple through life the rest of his days.

Ryman's shellackin' pains me terrible. If I had my druthers I'd grab Lon Warfield's pistol and shoot Bob Cleary 'tween the eyes, but Ryman would yell, "Stay outta my rock patch, Zee."

Sweaty palms and stingin' eyes be hanged, I gotta a job to do. So I climb into the Big Money seats to handle bettin' needs there. A soft-handed feller in a gray fedora, pushes two Abe's at me. I give him a marker, and grab five Washington's from a city boy with thick glasses and new shoes.

A farmer in the standin' section yells, "Dummy, get yer ass over here."

I duck under the rope and take the farmer's greenbacks. A quick glance shows Ryman layin' in the dust like a lazy dog. The farmer's bucks are probably all he has left from that load of hay he sold last fall, stashed them rolled up bills in a Prince Albert tobacco can in the barn rafters, should Baby Sister's headaches return and the doc needs to visit, or the vet gets called durin' calvin' season.

"Mark me for three bucks, Dummy. All Ryman's gonna win to-night is a trip to the cemetery."

I write, "3 bucks. Redheaded farmer. New overalls." on my paper, scrawl $3 on 'nother sheet and hand it to him. He'll get his money back, 'long with matching funds from Ryman's wad if Bob Cleary holds his gains, which I hope he don't.

For the fighters it's winner take all. Knock the other guy sense-less or make him cry uncle and the pot's yours. My cigar box is jammed with seven, eight hunnert bucks, not countin' Ryman's seed money.

Truth be told, folks are more 'n a little surprised at how this fan-dango's unfurled, even if they hoped it'd be this way. But, hope's one thing, and real somethin' different.

On the fight floor, Bob Cleary yells, "Get up, Old Man. I got more where that come from." Ryman pulls hisself to one knee, but looks like he ain't got the strength, nor juice, to spit.

* * *

Ridin' over from Yellowbird in Lon Warfield's pickup earlier this evenin', Ryman said, "These boys got money to burn. We have an obligation to see it goes in our pocket, so they won't start no unsafe fires."

That's Ryman. All jokes and razzin' 'cept when he's beatin' the sap outta some young man with more moolah than brains. He's lucky if he just gets knocked out. Some of Ryman's opponents limp through life after a go at Ryman. Some lose a eye, or get a broke back 'cause they get up after Ryman hammers 'em to the ground. One young man spends his days strapped to a chair, prayin' he won't pass out from the pain of his next spasm. Pride ain't got no place in the fight game.

In the fight ring, Bob Cleary struts, the prettiest rooster in the coop, hopin' Ryman gets up, so he can knock him from here to St. Louis and be rich as a bank robber from the prize money.

* * *

This fist throwin' contest come 'bout nigh onto two months ago. I brung a mess of fresh carrots onto the back porch. Ryman waves a envelope. "My answer to Cleary," he says. "I'll whup his ass the first Saturday in June. His bailiwick."

He thumbs a stamp on the letter. "Goin' by the post office the next day or two, Zee? Drop this off would ya?"

Since Ryman's doin' the askin', I whoop up my mule, Pete Grey, and clippety-clop into Yellowbird, where Miss Hattie McCormack, the post mistress, drops the letter into the mail bag. Miss Hattie's a special friend. She taught me to finger talk. My ears may be blistered and orange as a dried apricot, but I hear just fine. My talk box got burned away in the house fire that kilt sister Darcy and turned Pap to a black cinder, and scarred me good. The onlyist sounds I make are mouth noises, hisses, grunts and lip pops.

Some years past, Miss Hattie said, "I bought a book that shows how to spell words using fingers. If we both learn, you can use your fingers to make your needs known."

That were 'bout the time the schoolmarm said my scarred-ugly face made little ones pee their pants, and either I quit school, or she quits teachin'. Faced with that threat, it were no contest. I quit school, and Miss Hattie taught me to read and do sums, with me spellin' my answers on my fingers. That were a blessin' most as big as Ryman's generosity, I tell you.

Now, Miss Hattie asks, "Still planning to move to Jeff City and look for your Momma?"

I spell out, "Most likely. When Winder's in school."

She nods. "Good time as any to dig up old bones, I guess. Remember, just because your Momma was seen in the Katy railroad depot dressed to the high heavens doesn't mean she's a Katy Lady."

I nod. Soft words don't change hard facts. Mom liked her drink when she lived with me and Pap and Darcy, so bein' a Katy Lady fits her like a Saturday night dance. Katy Ladies comfort lonely men travelers on the railroad. The ladies ride free and share their earnin's with the conductor.

I spell out, "That's where I'll start."

Miss Hattie nods. "I'm here if you need me."

I nod, climb on Pete and kick him to a trot. I wanna get home and pick some tunes on my banjo to keep away bad thoughts.

* * *

When I first taken bed and founder with Ryman's family, they farmed 90 acres of Missouri River bottom land, south and east of Yellowbird. Dirt farmin's never easy, but the summer of '32, it got terrible. Them bankers at the Yellowbird National Bank stole his inheritance, nigh onto $9,000, and closed the bank for good. Come spring, the Ol' Muddy flooded for the fourth straight year and washed away everone of Ryman's crops. Money gets scarce when yer seeds, yer out buildin's, even yer cows, float downstream to New Orleans, leavin' piles of sand and bloated fish where tall corn oughta grow.

Toppin' off these miseries, Ryman's sweet wife, Miss Ethel, she who nursed me back to health when I were burned, passed away fall of '41, leavin' Ryman with three daughters and Winder to raise without a woman's touch. He come to Jeff City and brung me home. I been his cook and chore doer since.

Now, the fifth day of June, 1943, Bob Cleary parades like the King of Prussia, pretendin' he's the new bare knuckle champ of Callaway County. Come Saturday night he hopes to waltz into Yellowbird, the ladies smilin' all big, at him, each one eager to hop in the buggy and go for a ride. He just needs to salt Ryman Call away. That's all.

* * *

A little over two hours ago, Lon Warfield parked his pickup under the big maples next to the IGA warehouse. Ryman climbed out, stretched and touched his toes. Ten or twelve men boo like he's a Halloween ghost, hot as a railroad spike left in the sun for the local fighter.

"Yer jest a fart in a windstorm 'round here, Ryman," one yells.

'Nother hollers, "Yer dead an' don't know it. Lay down. Make it easy on the undertaker."

Ryman waves. "Sorry to ruin yer party, boys, but I'm gonna send yer feller home with his tail 'tween his legs." He laughs, but he's serious as sin.

Word that champion Ryman Call has arrived travels fast. 'Fore ya can say May, June and July, a dozen or so more fight fans hot-foot over from the Harvest Moon Bar. They figure Ryman'll get his ass kicked, but who don't want to gander at the king 'fore he's knocked from his throne?

Addin' sugar to the spice, the feller they figger to do the knockin' is a youngster they seen climb onto his momma's lap on Market Day, unbutton her dress, say "Tit" and suck. Don't that make Ryman's demise even more grand?

* * *

Me, Lon Warfield and 9-year-old Winder, my special charge at his Daddy's fights, are invisible to these folks. They eye Ryman like a prize bull when he crosses the parkin' lot and goes inside for the usual pre-fight confab.

Lon Warfield, Ryman's driver, melts into the crowd, pistol in his pocket. Ryman says, "Lon's quiet as a Indian and smart as a owl. He can gut and skin a deer 'fore it's last turd hits the ground."

Inside, Ryman ponies up a hunnert dollars to Tom Baker, the fight timekeeper. The local boy hands Tom five hunnert smackeroos for the honor of gettin' the hominy-grit shit beat outta him. Tom drops the Jing-a-ling into a bag and straps it to his leg where it'll stay 'til a clear winner's declared.

Fight fans from Columbia and Jeff City, mebbe even St. Louis, park Fords, Chevys, and Desotos, along the gravel road in front of the IGA Warehouse, come inside and wash down hamburgers and hotdogs with Griesedieck Brothers beer. They don't give a hang who wins this rumpus long as they got money on the winner. They wear blue or tan pants and white short-sleeve shirts open at the neck and smoke store-bought cigarettes.

The local boys hobble their wagon team in the pasture behind the warehouse, wearin' fresh-ironed overalls and blue shirts, heavy shoes or boots wiped clean of cow manure and horse dust. They're bettin' the neighbor boy beats the royal shit out of Ryman Call tonight and if they take a fiver, mebbe even a ten-spot home to the little lady, that ain't no sin, right?

After Ryman agreed to this shindig, he learned Bob Cleary were fifteen years younger, five inches taller and mebbe fifty pounds heavier'n him. "He hits like a fallin' tree, with arms long as a mowin' blade. His last three fights, he knocked out good men in less than seven minutes. Total. He's got sparkle."

Ryman laughs. "Good fer him. A good fight means a happy crowd and folks eager for our next knuckle-throwin' party. That's more greenback dollars for my family."

Ryman'll fight a giant and two midgets at the same time, if the money's right. Tonight, he's got to handle this big, strong man in his own backyard, with the crowd yellin' encouragement ever breath he takes, ever fist he throws. That's a heavy load even for champion Ryman Call.

For Cleary, this fight's like candy from Santa Claus. Hell, Ryman's old enough to be his daddy. *He's gonna get whupped sometime, so why not tonight?* Winnin' the pot is the difference 'tween drivin' a Farmall tractor come plowin' time, or lookin' a sway-backed mule in the ass 'nother year. Plus, Cleary aims to ladle gravy on his taters from side bets won from them who don't think he's got the goods to handle Ryman Call.

As the never been whupped top dog in the county, Ryman names where the fight's to be held and when. Ryman don't fight in Yellowbird, 'cause he knows even for them that been there afore, crows get lost lookin' for our slice of Heaven. We got more hills than hollers, and if the road ain't washed out and muddy it's rocky, with so many twists and turns you think you're goin' forward, when you're really goin' backards.

As to fight time for tonight's get go, Ryman named twenty-minute rounds with a five-minute blow in between. If both fighters still stand after all that fist-throwin', they take ten minutes to piss and gulp down a beer or two, then battle 'til one of 'em quits or goes down and stays down.

The rules agreed to, I tag along when Ryman walks the warehouse, Winder holdin' my thumb like a chicken leg. *I'll miss that boy when I'm gone, I tell you.*

Sawdust is spread on the fresh-oiled wood floor that smells like smoke and kerosene. Two yellow light bulbs dangle from black cords in the center of the room where the gladiators come to mark. A cellar door, two hickory saplin's nailed 'cross it, leans agin the far wall, transportation to the sawbones, if needed, and most fighters, need it after Ryman's busted 'em up good.

Healthy young ladies with big bosoms sell dime hot dogs and hamburgers, washed down with 15-cent beer from booths roped off agin the wall. Wood benches form a square where the fighters mix it up toward the center of the room. If ya ain't got a buck for a bench seat up front, four bits buys ya a place to stand, clean to the wall on both sides. Jake Atteberry, the IGA store owner, oughta slip Ryman a Franklin or two since the hope that Ryman'll get his ass whupped is why folks have piled in here, thick as thieves.

After the walk-through, me and Winder follow Ryman to Lon's pick up where Ryman changes into tight black pants with a red cloth belt and high-top canvas shoes. He trots up the road a hunnert yards or so and back, a bevy of school boys runnin' long side, chatterin' like blue jays.

"I'm gonna be a fighter when I grow up." And, "Knock the shit outta him, Mr. Call."

Back at the truck, Ryman does jumpin' jacks, dabs Vaseline on his eyebrows, 'round his ears and nose, slicks his red hair back with pomade and trots to the fight place. I pocket the Vaseline for later use, help Winder shoulder his Daddy's stool, and carry Ryman's ice bucket and towels. Winder walks by my side.

When Ryman enters the fight place, fight fans yell cat calls at him. "Ya'll look like that freak next to ya 'fore the night's over." That's meant for me, but don't bother me none. I know I'm ugly. 'Nother yell is, "Don't worry, Ryman. We'll take good care of ya. We got a hearse outside."

When the local hero marches in, the crowd cheers. He has a I-hate-the-world-look on his whiskered face. He's monster big, mebbe 6 foot 4 or 5, a solid 250-260. His hair is bushy and black as a wolverine's, his squinty eyes, ice blue.

Ryman shuffles his feet in sawdust, then hustles out to the mark. Cleary comes up. He wears long underwear cut off at the waist and cinched with a wide leather belt, the drop seat sewed shut. He's bare-chested. Standin' next to him, Ryman looks like a lost school boy. Ryman says to Cleary, "Yer last will and testament wrote, Shorty?"

The gong sounds. The big bruiser pops Ryman with a hard right. Ryman fires a straight left to let folks know he come to the dance. Cleary is a southpaw, a fighter who leads with his right hand. Ryman ain't seen this style 'fore, so his guard ain't good as it should be. Cleary's jabs sound horsewhip loud agin Ryman's face and arms. When Ryman hits him, Cleary grunts.

Ryman says, "Lookin' for yer Momma? Try the cheek. She's showin' her hairy thang to the men a dime a look." He hopes this will rile the young fighter, so he'll throw wild punches and wear hisself out. Cleary just grins.

Round one ends. Neither fighter has a clear advantage, but things change faster than a left jab in round two. The big boy is on Ryman like dust on a tobacco plant.

I 'spec Ryman's put out by this, 'cause most fights he knocks some poor sucker out while the gong still quivers, then chugs beer in the tavern, his winnin's piled on the bar, eyein' the local talent, decidin' which lucky girl he'll court tonight.

Tonight's merry-go-round is a hump and a holler from Ryman's first lollapalooza. That were one Saturday night at the Pick and Shovel Bar in Mokane. Ryman was enjoyin' a cold beer after a hard week's work. Them two Hatton brothers marched in. They pointed at a certain farmer's wife, sayin' they'd sure like a go with her and her sittin' right there next to her husband eatin' a cheeseburger.

When her man rose to speak, Tim Hatton busted the farmer's nose wide open, hammered him to the floor and kicked in his ribs. This riled Ryman, who seen the whole thing.

He told Tim Hatton he were wrong usin' language like that in front of a lady, and to apologize. Tim said, "Make me. Old Man."

His brother, Tom, laughed. "We do what we want. Any old man who don't like that better mind his own bidness or be ready to get the Shinola beat outta him."

Ryman said, "So that's the way it is, huh?" He turned like he were gonna walk away, then wheeled and fired two punches. Both brothers skidded slammed agin booth clear 'cross the room, out cold as a lantern with no oil.

Tom Baker got wind of this little tussle. Tuesday evenin' he come callin'. He told Ryman they was a challenge fight in Jeff City that comin' Saturday night. Ryman said he'd give it a go, since twenty bucks would buy his girls new winter clothes.

Saturday night, Ryman's punch 'bout ripped his opponent's head off his shoulders. He brung home most onto thirty bucks, after he given some to Tom Baker for the tip. Tom hisself made some serious moola when his side bets were on Ryman.

The followin' week, at Tom's urgin', Ryman signed on for a six-man Free-for-All. This where each fighter puts a ten spot in the pot. The last one standin' wins it all. "Fifty dollars buys my seed come plantin' time," Ryman said.

Tom Baker pocketed a ten spot from the bar owners for bossin' the whole affair, plus a buck from each fighter for his timekeepin'. He done right good bettin' Ryman would clean everone's plow, and he did. Since that night, Tom time-keeps at all of Ryman's fights.

Eddie Kepler and his wife Claudette, got wind there was gonna be fist throwin' party. It must of seemed like feather bed money to them, since Eddie all the time bragged he could knock over a outhouse with a blow from his big fist. That prize money would buy new suckers for they's well pump, and Claudette cottoned a new red dress from J.C. Penney. And new lipstick.

'Fore they left home, they took ten rainy-day smackeroos from the Clabber Girl Baking Soda can on the top shelf in the kitchen cabinet, and dropped it into the jar on the bar at the Wise Owl in Ashland. Eddie were sure he'd be found a fast road to riches when he knocked out the local butcher his first fight.

In his second go 'round, Eddie laid out the preacher's son with two punches. When Eddie seen his next opponent were Ryman Call, his eyes lit up, convinced this would be a duck soup go for him. After all, Ryman were probably forty-years old, and Eddie just turned twenty-five.

'Fore the fight, Eddie sidled up to Ryman. "I got a ten spot that says I whup yer ass, Old Man. Can ya match it?"

The way side bets 'tween fighters are usually handled, is the timekeeper holds the money and pays the winner. When Eddie didn't follow these rules, Ryman grinned, figurin' Eddie didn't have the gettis to back his bet.

"Yer on, Youngster," Ryman said.

Tom Baker hits the gong. Eddie comes out swingin'. Ryman swats his blows away like they was smoke rings, then slaps Eddie like a daddy does to correct his boy. This angrified Eddie. He commenced to throw rights and lefts that miss Ryman here to Minnesota. After mebbe five minutes, his face welted and red from Ryman's slaps, pantin' like a dog chasin' rabbits, sweat drippin from his chin,' Eddie drops his guard.

Ryman slaps him twice more. Hard. Eddie stands still as a fence post. Ryman tousles his hair like he were a youngster, then unloads a right to his chin. Bones snap. Blood flies. Eddie falls.

Ten minutes and two buckets of cold water later, he sits up, spits out a tooth and asks, "Where am I?"

"In my shit house," Ryman says. "Where's my ten bucks?"

His lips bloody and swole up like a dead cow left in the sun, Eddie whines, "Mr. Call, could ya kindly give me a few days? I'll sell a load of wood or somethin' to pay what I owe."

Ryman says, "Sure, I could do that. But, I won't. If I did, I'd have forty-seven challenges in three minutes from every asshole with two fists and no money in his pocket. You made the bet, boy. Pay up."

"Wouldja take my mules?"

"Naw, I got a good team. 'Sides, how'd ya plow come spring?"

Eddie don't answer.

Ryman says, "Got a cow?"

Eddie shakes no.

"Too, bad," Ryman says.

Ryman eyes Claudette, Eddie's wife, who's wipin' blood from her husband's face, her face white as a rag. "Ya countenance his bet," Ryman asks.

Claudette flutters blue eyes at Ryman. "No sir. He does stupid things on his own." She pushes a blonde curl behind her ear.

Ryman says. "Eddie, yer wife worth ten bucks?"

Eddie lets out a long breath. Claudette waits for Eddie to answer, a smile on her red lips. When Eddie don't open his yap, she says, "Ya damn right, I am. Got a car? Or will our wagon bed do?"

* * *

Good fighters don't beg. For years, Ryman Call's beat the goose feathers off ever fighter he's faced, but tonight he's gettin' pay back. He's got two choices. One, stay in the sawdust and not come to mark the next round, so that Bob Cleary wins the pot, or he can get up and Bob Cleary creams him. That's how his cards stack up.

Bob Cleary, on his part, celebrates like it's his birthday, certain the fight's over. He blows kisses to the crowd and does backflips, shakes his fist at Ryman and jigs.

While he's doin' all this, Ryman scrambles on all fours to the far corner of the fight floor, and stands, his guard up. There's more'n one way to de-nut a hog, he figgers.

Cleary spies Ryman and comes runnin'. "Yer mine, Old Man, yer mine."

Ryman greets Bob with a straight left to the jaw and a right to the heart, but his punches ain't got snap. He uses rasslin' holds to keep Cleary off balance 'til the gong sounds.

Cleary skips back to his stool, happy as a schoolgirl. He punches the air mebbe fifty times, certain he'll knock Ryman into next week when the gong sounds. His brothers pound his back and call him "Champ," eager for the fight purse and side bet money to fill they's pockets. All that's left is for Bob to coldcock Ryman. That's all.

* * *

Ryman slumps on his stool, dusty as a railroad hobo, blood oozin' from a cut over his right eye. He watches Cleary celebrate. "Go ahead, boy," he whispers. "Wear yerself out."

Ryman pulls me close. "Any idees?"

I shake no. I ain't a corner man like boxin' glove fighters have, a fight-smart feller who stops blood from a cut and gives his fighter advice. I can't talk, much less make swellins' go down. And who am I to tell Ryman how to fight? He needs to get his piss and vinegar back to win this little quarrel.

Ryman has 'nother problem. If he lasts 'nother round, he'll have to fight 'til him or Cleary go down and stay down. That ain't good. Ryman's right eye is swole up like wasps held a stingin' contest on him, his chest and arms covered with red welts and purple bruises. Sawdust sticks to his shoulders. He's wet from sweat. He'll piss claret for a week.

Will tonight be the first time ever Ryman Call don't come to scratch, his time as champion ended?

Winder stands soldier-straight behind his Daddy's stool, his fists clenched, his knuckles white, fightin' tears. Lon Warfield pushes through the crowd to gander at Ryman. His face goes pale. He don't speak, just turns and heads outside to see the moon, rather than watch Ryman get knocked silly.

Ryman Call's the best man I've ever knowed. He found me cold, wet and bad burned and he brung me home. His wife, Miss Ethel, patched me up. Since that day to this, some seven years have passed. I've slept under Ryman's roof and filled my belly at his table. Now, he's a goner, and they's no help I can give him.

* * *

Ryman pulls me close. "Think I outta use my crippled quail?"

What Ryman means is, he'll act like one of Cleary's punches hurts him bad, the way a momma quail pretends she has a broke wing when you get too close to her babies. She'll flutter 'long the ground just outta reach. When you've followed her fifteen or twenty feet, and her brood's safe, her wings gets a magic cure and off she flies, fast as a Indian arrow. That's what Ryman means.

I nod, and poke the air with my right and fire a left. Ryman says,

"Gotcha. I ain't thrown a decent one all night."

The crowd commences to laugh. I turn. Two boys, one dressed like a scarecrow, the other like a old woman, stand near me.

"Yer a ugly son-a-bitch," Scarecrow says.

I can't argue. It's true. Folks suspicion the fire that scarred me bad was started by my own momma on purpose, since she ain't been seen in these parts since that night. 'til last month when she were spied at the Katy station in Jeff City.

I offer my hand to Scarecrow, like his joke's fun. He tosses a cup of liquid at me. By the smell, it's coal oil. The Old Woman's match flames out 'fore it catches fire. Folks slap they's knees and laugh. It ain't funny to me.

Now, I know I gotta find my momma and learn if she started the fire that killed Darcy and Pap.

A fight fan from the big money seats hustles up, grabs the boys and pulls 'em outside. "Idiots," he says. "You'll burn the whole place down."

Ryman says, "Pay 'em no mind, Zee."

Easy for him to say, but it's me they made laughin' stock of.

Winder says, "Ya ain't ugly, Hamas. And yer sure nice to me."

That may be true, but I gotta face my past.

The gong sounds. Round five. Bob Cleary rushes out, eyes gleamin', ready to put Ryman asleep. He fires punches like they cancelled tomorrow and he's the onlyist one to know it. Ryman grabs him and holds on, so Bob's fists hit only his arms and shoulders. Bob's blows don't seem to have steam like earlier. *Did he celebrate too much?*

Ryman lands a right hook to Cleary's belly. Cleary backs off, probably surprised at Ryman's get up and go. Me, too. Then, Ryman slaps Cleary. The crowd roars. They know this is Ryman sayin' settle yer bets boys, I got the reins. This fight's mine.

Cleary's eyes go big. He flings a right. Ryman blocks it and slaps him agin. Cleary charges Ryman like a Arkansas razorback goin' for a slop trough.

Ryman dances away. Cleary's left glances his shoulder. Ryman slaps Cleary agin.

"Ya dumb sonavabitch," Cleary yells. He fires 'nother right, 'nother left, 'nother right but hits only air.

"Stand still," he yells at Ryman.

Cleary zings a left, a right, a left. Ryman blocks 'em all. Cleary's eyes glint like a badger chasin' a chicken. He fires a long right to Ryman's forehead. Ryman goes down like he were shot. Cleary yells, "Get up, Ol' man. I'm gonna wreck ya!"

Cleary waves to the crowd, and hops 'round like a grasshopper on a fryin' pan. Ryman drags hisself to the far corner of the fight floor, and stands, wavin' like a persimmon sprout in the wind. Cleary rushes him. Ryman feints with his right. Bob Cleary's eyes follow this fist for a hiccup, after all that's where Ryman's poison is.

Ryman's left hook sizzles in over Cleary's right shoulder and smashes agin his jaw. Cleary's mouth pops open. Teeth spill into the dirt. Blood spurts.

It's hard to knock out a man as big as Bob Cleary with one punch. Ryman knows time's runnin' out, but he can't hurry. He sends a hard right to Cleary's nose. The sound of snapped bone causes fight fans to flinch. Blood gushes from Cleary's face like tomatoes from a jar. Ryman's left sends him to the sawdust.

Cleary gazes up at Ryman, his mouth open. He shakes his head to chase away this bad dream. A short breath earlier, Ryman Call were the one down. Now, probably wagon wheels float 'fore Cleary's eyes, the salty blood fillin' his mouth.

Cleary staggers to his feet. Ryman bangs a right hook to his kidney. Can Ryman finish Cleary 'fore the gong sounds?

Cleary lunges at Ryman. He knows his neighbor's bet good money sayin' he'd win this scuffle, money to buy a new calf, or shingle the smokehouse. He wants one clear punch at Ryman, so they can collect their bets and go home rich. He probably hates the place where minutes earlier, he were king.

"Stand still, Coward," he yells at Ryman.

Standin' by his stool, Cleary's brothers are helpless as 'possums in a tree. One kneels, chewin' the towel he waved a short minute ago. The older brother closes his eyes, but that don't stop the sound of that son-of-a-bitch Ryman Call firing punch-after-punch into Brother's broken body.

The crowd's quiet as a church at collection time. They came to see the new king crowned, not watch him get beat bloody. Why'd I bet agin Ryman, they probably ask. Now, like water poured on fresh-plowed ground, that money's gone, 'long with the new garden plow and hog wire fence.

Bob Cleary's arms dangle at his side. Blood covers his chest and belly. He turns from the waist to follow Ryman's moves. Tom Baker, raises his hammer, ready to signal the fight's end.

Ryman pops Cleary with a hard right. Yet Cleary stands, a gnarled tree with strong roots. Ryman rears back to deliver a mighty blow. Instead, he shoves Cleary, who staggers, twists and falls. Ryman catches him and lowers him to the sawdust like he's layin' one of his precious daughters into bed for a long sleep.

The gong sounds. Cleary's brothers run out to carry him to his stool. "Ya win, ya son-of-a-bitch," the older brother says. "Bob's had 'nuff."

The crowd mutters like pigeons in a coop, bumpin' shoulders as they push out of the fight place, air smellin' like a over-turned privy. It ended so fast, some don't know what happened. One minute, the great Ryman Call was down. The next, they's hero's a sawdust-covered lump on the floor.

"Did Ryman fire a left and a right, or two lefts," a man asks his neighbor. Some of the big city boy's face is pale, like they have a touch of ague comin' on.

At Lon's truck, Ryman pays Tom Baker ten dollars for his time-keepin', plus a fiver for gas. He probably made 'nother fifty or sixty on side bets. Tom's wife is a Baptist, so he'll head home. Ryman'll settle with Lon Warfield later.

Ryman says, "That left ya suggested started his downfall, Zee. Had to damn near kill him 'fore he went down." He shakes his head. "Ain't this a nasty game? Beat someone 'til they can't walk, just for money."

He's never said anything like that 'fore now. Ryman towels

blood off and changes into clean overalls and shirt. I rub Vaseline on cuts over his eyes and stow his fight gear in Lon's truck, grab my banjo and follow him and Winder to the Harvest Moon bar. We ain't got no bets to settle, since we won 'em all.

Inside the tavern, the music box plays Bob Wills and his Texas Playboys', *Please Don't Leave Me.* Folks stand on the dance floor. They clear a path when Ryman comes up. A girl in a flowered skirt and red high heels stands on tip toes to kiss Ryman's black eye. "I'll take good care of ya," she says.

"You're a pretty thing," Ryman says, giving her a squeeze. As he walks mebbe ten young men grab at him. A boy in a white shirt and straw hat says, "Won me forty-three dollars tonight, Mr. Call. Much obliged."

"Good for you," Ryman says. "'Bout what I'm takin' home. But ya got yer's without spillin' a drop of blood." Everone laughs.

We climb onto bar stools. Roy Acuff's *Beautiful Brown Eyes* plays on the jukebox. The sweet scent of Midnight in Paris perfume mixes with cigarette smoke and beer. A pretty redhead stands kissin' close to Ryman.

"Hear you're quite a dancer," she says.

Ryman touches his swollen eye. "Not tonight, honey. 'Nother time I'll show you a few moves."

She smiles and rolls her big brown eyes.

I drink red soda pop while Winder guzzles Dr. Pepper. Ryman drains his Griesedieck, and stands. "Let's go, boys. Been a long night."

Me and Winder climb into Lon's pick up, and pull the tarp to our neck. Winder rests his head on my shoulder. He's asleep 'fore we cross the railroad tracks. Stars fill the sky. The air is warm and heavy, but I shiver and shake all the way home.

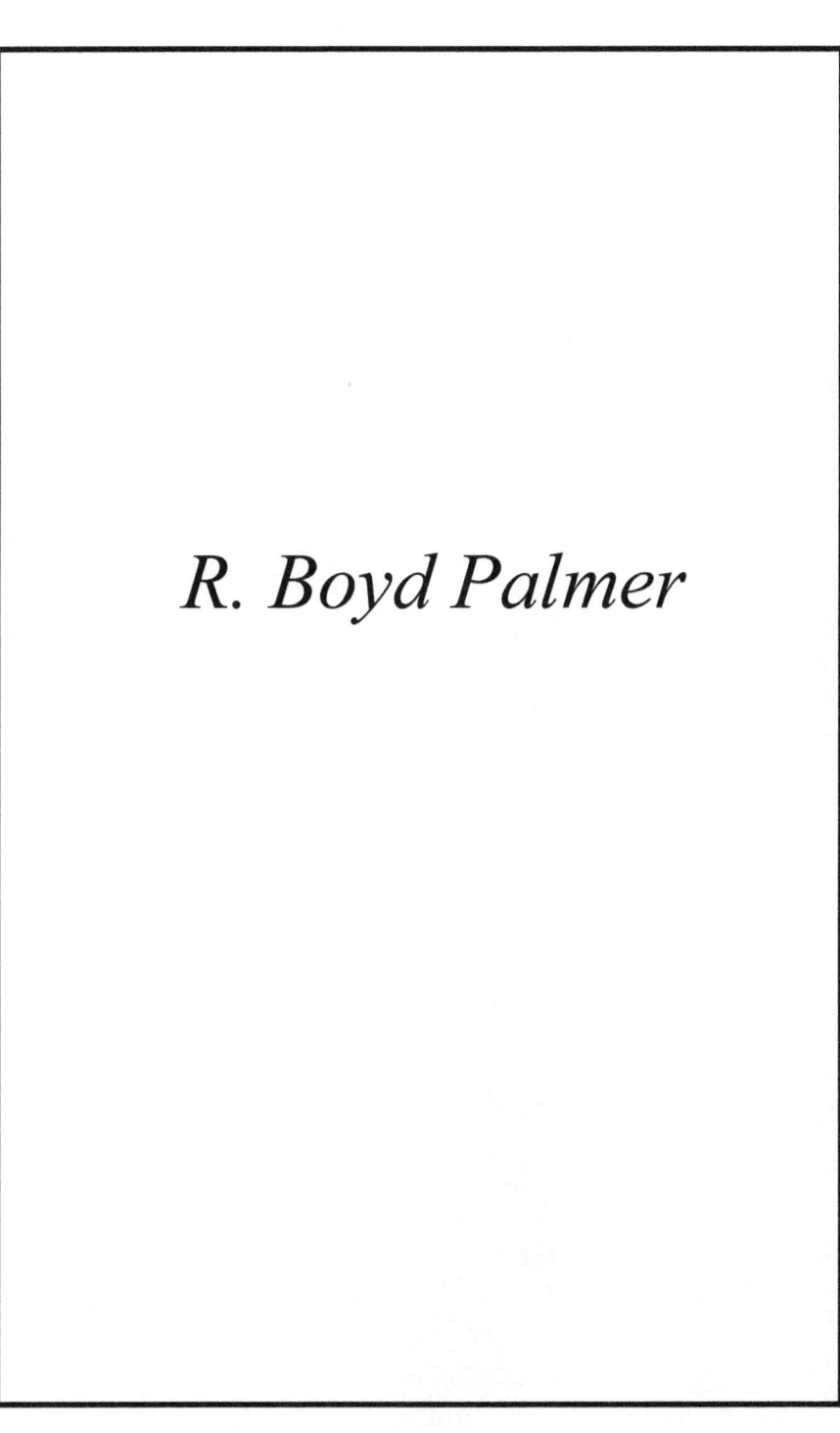

R. Boyd Palmer

Baraka Appears

I dream that I awake
to a whinny
And Baraka stands
by the bed.

I grab a handful of mane–
Throw a leg up over
his bare brown back–
and off go we with the wind.

He has his head—
I'd not thought to bridle.
I feel as free as does he–
Just Baraka and me and the ride.

That familiar feel as he gathers
himself for each stride–
Then thrown forward am I
by his power of thrust
into the flow of his reach.

In full motion now he moves like a deer.
Fluid as silk, smooth as slick satin.
I laugh as he whinnies
and bounds into the blue–

Hey, wait a minute. Horses don't fly.
I know where you came from.
She sent you to get me.
Your home's there in heaven now too.

The Dick Halligan Quartet

Sounds!
like I never heard…
touching me places I'd forgotten I'd known.

A drum man playing my bones with his sticks.
A saxophone that grabbed me—
rose the hair *all the way up my spine*
sssshhheewwwww
And all I was drinking was orange juice and soda.

And the guy on bass…hunched like a gorilla
sleeves rolled up
Long thick fingers playing strings
And it wasn't the bass he was playing
it was me…in a language from an ancient time.

A jungle-deep primal drum
Bing Bang Bong Boom
A chest thumping in the dark of night
calling me out…

JAZZZ!! Like I never heard before…
Who knew they could tune drums like that?!
Change skins… Put fibre in the sound…

And Halligan on piano…he writes the stuff.
It's orchestrated! They're reading music!
A score with room to play around, so it's alive!

Ohhhh that music…those sounds and rhythms
played inside me…under my skin…I was *alive*…
and you, my love, warm in the curve of my arm…
should've seen your face…the way you looked at me.
We were alive for each other that night.

Empty Arms

On the edge of dream I hear a Mourning Dove.
As I awake my arms reach for you
and you're not there.
Then I remember, you are gone

And nevermore will my arms hold you.
But they listen not to me and search the bed.
My fingers find your pillow and pull it close.
My arms make believe it's you.
My heart does too.

Oh, my body *yearns* for yours to hold.
Finger tips tingle to trace your lips lightly
and have them turn into a smile
That dazzles me, with the mystery of you.

Oh how I've loved you *and* love you still.
I long for the sight and the fragrance of you
and to feel your soft breath in my ear,
as you whisper those things I most need to hear.

The Day Don Romero Died

Today it's eight months you are gone.
The days are too short,
the nights so long.

I feel like Baraka, his first night alone
on the day Don Romero died...remember?

Back and forth along the fence
he rushed and whinnied
calling his buddy to *come home*.

It wasn't until later,
long after dark
I heard him chewing his hay.

He's now gone the same as you,
and left alone as twilight settles
to deep purple gloom...
I'm calling *you* to come home.

Feed Your Heart

The sprightly silver-haired shaman,
enchantment in her tone, implores
of the small circle
gathered 'round her in the glen:

"Call forth the light and the darkness
and look deeply into shadows.
It must be there somewhere,
that which you seek…

"Always empty, never full
a traveling appetite.
Constantly in need.
Always hungry.

"Never whole.
Never complete.
Something always missing.
What could it be?"

"Love," answers a little girl.

"You think…?" the old woman smiles.

"I know," says the child, "nothing
else fills you up. You take a
full tummy to bed with you,
but your heart is empty all night."

The shaman smiles at the young girl
and speaks to the hungry faces,

"Listen to the child. Feed your heart."
And her smile, embraces them all.

Looking Down

I look down, see my feet on the ground
Then as in a dream, when I close my eyes
I'm high up, way up here in the top of a
still unfinished structure—
amidst a tangle of cable and wire
Hanging on with one hand
and it's a long way down.

Weak with the fear of falling I
look at the white knuckled grip
on which I depend—and with
sudden horror, become aware of *something
somewhere* in me, that just might let go.

I look to find where I can wrap arms around something
not have to keep hanging on by one hand alone.
Where is my other hand?
...and then I know. It has already let go...

First Night Of Summer

I dream I'm in a place unknown to me.
Lost my shirt. Am looking for it.
Checking the lower portion of a bunk bed
…can't find it.

See thru an open door, or an archway,
my car out there in the square
…head for it.

The atmosphere as I approach is
of a slightly sinister carnival. Men
standing and sitting about,
silently watching me.

For safety, I maintain a proper
tension of mood and movement.
Reach into my left pants pocket …
Come up with glittering
golden, ornate keys on a ring…
they aren't mine. Give them to
one of the men standing near as I pass.
Continue to find more, golden
and ornate as I search.

Finally down under a folded wad of tissue at
the very bottom of my pocket, I feel my keys.
Pull them out and as I look they begin to shimmer
…transfixed and entranced by sparkle; can't see clearly,

I close my eyes and rely on the touch of my fingers.
By feel I can tell they're mine. My thumbnail
engages and slightly spreads the spiral ring I know so well
…and in mind's eye see its worn and tarnished, silvery look.

Which key on the ring is for the car? Not sure and the tension
around me is growing. I open my eyes to look, but the flickering
confuses me…

I hold the keys in my hand. No need to look anymore
…but which one is it will open the door?
Put me in the driver's seat and fit the ignition
—before it all turns ugly?

Then grown of a sudden quiet and still
a gentle voice speaks in me,
Choose by the feel of it…
you'll know in your heart
what to do…

The Zoo

Man threw himself a curve
and caught it.
Told himself a lie
and bought it.

And the monkeys all laughed
in the zoo...

He came from the ape
for heavens sake;
Even the gorilla
knows that.

Who ever thought
there'd come a day
when the wild would
be treated this way?

That Almighty Monkey,
on-high in his tree,
has plenty to answer for
believe you me.

OH, I know. I know. But we
all know it's **true**...
He should never have
put man
in charge of the zoo.

When I Was Three

Wouldn't listen–
didn't know how
to be good.

Mommy would say,
"Someday, you'll be sorry,
when I'm dead and gone..."

Every night
on my knees I'd pray,
"Please, God...

don't let mommy die,
before me."

Then one night–
I'm just playing.
Having fun...

She says,
"If you don't stop
teasing your baby brother

–I'm going to leave and
you'll never see me again."

I just laugh…
She's said that lots of times
and never left me.

But of a sudden she
dries her hands
on the dish towel–

takes off her apron
folds it
puts it by the sink.

Goes to the clothes-tree
by the door to outside,
Puts on her sweater,

Opens the door, and
walks out, into the dark!

I look at father
still sitting at the table
in his undershirt reading the paper.

He doesn't even care, I think,
and a chill touches me
thru the cellar door

where he'd taken
my dog Jerry down–
chained him to the furnace

–and shot him dead
for killing chickens.

Father *tried* to teach him.
Even hung a dead one
'round his neck.

Jerry had to eat and sleep with it,
'til it started to smell

–but he still wouldn't *mind,*

–just like me,
didn't know *how*
to be good

and I feel something stir
down there in the dark—
waiting...

My baby brother begins to cry–
I go to him.

Help him onto my lap.
We hug–
Maybe he can sleep with me tonight,
I think.

Then I hear the door open–
And what looks like Mommy
walks in!

–but she *isn't* my mommy.
My Mommy'd *never* leave me!

That Mommy *I once* knew?
I'll never *see her* again!
...just like she said.

Outlaws

The young man in his top-down studmobile
with flashing eyes and flying locks speeds by.

My heart smiles and presses on the gas
while my gray-haired mind
looks out for black and white.

From my bad-guy good-guy mind
for the moment I am free.

And there's no outlaws here
there's only him and me.

Love On The Road

I am love here on the black-top.
The kiss and the whisper
where rubber meets the road.

It is a grind down here
but, we don't mind the pain.

"We're in love with the road,"
sing the tires.
"And I'm in love with you,"
whispers the road.

And all the while don't you know–

It is love up here at the wheel.
Window rolled down listening
to the song the tires sing.

In love with the road too.
Same as you.

Equanimity

Clumsier than I used to be
Constantly knocking things over…

And sometimes,
In some everyday simple move
I'll slip or skip a cog–
And suddenly everything's all outta whack.

Just a bit ago sitting at the computer,
Reaching to answer the phone
Rolling forward with my chair–
My stomach closed the keyboard drawer,
on which
my mid-day snack was perched–

A bowl of fresh ripe strawberries
I'd cleaned and cut.
Organic and beautiful
with creamy yogurt and coconut milk–

Hurled bounced and splashed
all over me and the chair.
running down
into
the delicate soft folds
of the seat…

Coming to rest in final slow pirouette
on goblet-like foot and stem of bowl
reclining now on floor–
Silver vessel shining up at me
as the last of its content
seeps…

I'd only had a bite before the phone rang.
Which by the way I answered.
A recorded message for seniors.
Sat there and listened...
Some gibberish about protecting me…

I don't need protection. Need an overhaul–
new wiring, I stand up look at the mess I've made–

Let out a "Son-of-a-bitch," a time or two–
"Damn it," once or twice
and end with "aww Fuck…"

That's it. Then I get rags, a large pan, hot water
and clean it up. Take off my pants, shirt, underwear,
which I put on clean this morning,
and throw them in the washing machine…
There ya have it, a day in the life of an elder.

No tears shed over spilt milk these days.
Just a bellow, a four letter word or two perhaps;
not directed at me or anyone else,
just to let it out and let it go.
Then clean up the mess…

And as I clean sometimes…it's like
cleaning Bart's litter box every day.
Makes me feel better.
So much crap in the world
I can't do anything about.
Well here's some I can.

Maybe on some level
I'm creating these messes for myself–
payback. Karma for all the messes I made
in life I *didn't* clean up.

When my debt's paid maybe
I'll be graced and shown a way to help
in the Sisyphean task of getting
this rock of ages to the next plateau.
The paradigm shift already in the making?

Only Teasing

The two men from the coroner's office prepare to leave the small bedroom on the second floor of the old clap-board house. "Alright, alright you can keep her tonight Mr. Deffenbacker," says the older of the two as they move toward the door, the worn, bare floor creaking under their weight, "but we'll be back in the morning to get her. You needn't see us out. We can find our way." He closes the door and as they make their way down the stairs, says under his breath to his partner, "Poor son-of-a-bitch. Half out of his mind..."

In the bedroom, Mumford Deffenbacker perches on the edge of his chair, attentive as a large bird of prey. On the bed is sprawled, the small, wet body of his wife, newly drowned in the canal. As the men let themselves out downstairs, a stillness settles on the house. He leans forward and pokes her with a meaty, calloused finger.

"Wake up, Sheila," he whispers. "Goddamn it now you got those other people fooled but not me. You're just trying to spite me; same as that stroke bullshit last year." He jabs her again, hard. "I'm warning you, Sheila, I've had enough of this shit now. I had a hard day, and I gotta come home and put up with this crap." He was crying now. "What in the hell is the matter with you? You want them to come tomorrow and take you away? You wanna be nailed in a box and get buried in the ground? Huh? Is that what you want?" He sits back and wipes his eyes with his fingers. "Alright, I'm gonna let 'em do it. See how you like it there. See how you like all that quiet and that dark. You're gonna be all alone, there won't be nobody to hear you when you decide to stop all the bullshit. Who you gonna have to tease you then, huh?"

That's it! That's what he'd do! Their old game; he'd play their old game! He moves to the edge of his chair and smiles as he stares at the twisted arm. He moves his gaze to the mouth turned down at one corner. Still smiling he emits a piercing, bird-like trill, "bbrreep. bbrreep."

He'd started the game last year, a few weeks after she came home from the hospital. It was a good game and although she'd never let on, he figured he knew she deserved it. If she was going to play her game with the arm and the mouth and the harsh, difficult voice she deserved to be teased for them. "Bbrreep, bbrreep," he teases as he smiles mockingly at the small, still figure.

He waits for her reaction; the squirming self-conscious move to hide her arm and turn her mouth away. As he waits… the stillness in the room begins to isolate him. He begins to feel alone. Alone, in a way he's never felt before. He stares at the small figure on the bed. *Something is missing. Something is gone.* Something he'd never even noticed was there before is gone. Why hadn't he ever noticed it?! *What was it?* Then he knew… "You're not Sheila," he accuses. "You're her body. Where's Sheila? What's happened to Sheila? Where'd she go??"

He moves to the bed and straightens the thin arms and legs. "Sheila? Please come back. I didn't mean it." he cries, "I didn't know." He brushes the matted hair from her face. "You're all wet. I'll get a towel."

The neatly hanging towels in the bathroom bring a lump to his throat. She was always so neat and clean about everything. The bathroom smells of lavender. He grabs the towels and rushes back to the bed. He tears the thin cotton dress down the front and pulls it from her. He throws the clothing across the room and begins to rub the white, wet body. With both hands he vigorously dries her.

"I'll get you warm, Sheila. I know how you always hated being cold. I'll take care of you. I won't let them take you and put you in the cold ground."

He takes off his heavy work shoes and lies down beside her. He gathers her in his arms and gently rocks her back and forth; holding her close; his cheek against hers. He hasn't held her like this in years; years that could've been so different if he'd only known; seen what now he knows and sees. Why was he so blind?

"You're so cold," he breathes into her ear, "oh Sheila, I'm so sorry for everything. I just didn't know. I thought you were spiting me. Why didn't you tell me?"

The pain is deeper than he's ever known. "I never knew you felt like this." He begins to sob, realizing how alone she must have been, to drown herself in the cold winter water of the canal.

Artie

He stood hunched over the old oak bar of the Mermaid Inn, listening to the sea running on the beach below. He knew all her voices and most of her moods. On land seven days now, his rum-cast mind was beginning to play tricks on him.

He cocked his grizzled head to the siren spell of liquid laughter. He hadn't heard her sound like this since that summer night off the Azores; when becalmed and crazed with an ancient longing he dove from the ship and followed her call. He never knew how much later it was she cast him up on a gentle beach...exhausted and at peace.

Now, a renewed peal of laughter brings him back to the present. He pushes his lean, hard body, arms length from the bar...all senses alert. As the barroom door swings wide, from across the room he sees her. She has size and she has grandeur and the old longing is upon him. Straightening to his full five foot five, Artie gets his sea legs under him and sets a level course through the tilting room...her laughter a sparkling lure.

Finding himself before her; from the dizzying heights of her breasts he squints up into eyes the color of deepwater, her large dimpled face surrounded by shimmering red haze, and in slack-jawed admiration speaks, "God help me, I ain't never seen nothin' like you before..."

"Hell, Cap'n, you're quite a sight yourself," she says, enveloping him in folds of powdered flesh, her rolling laughter sounding to his depths.

Hours later, as the sun slips into the sea, Millie settles into bed, gracefully as a ship entering water. She flows onto her back filling the bed with three-hundred pounds of perfumed undulations...beams a large wet smile at Artie, "Come on in, lover, the water's fine."

Artie stands on the foot of the bed, sets his sights, takes his bearings, this is an uncharted world. The breakers of her thighs whisper secrets of the deep; of voyages taken, adventures dreamed. She is a siren call and she is woman. He, a rising, howling wind as he climbs to the task...rigged for battle...The ocean can afford her excess, but the true sailor, the lover of the sea, has need to be spare.

With both hands on his manly tiller, he tacks into the storm. The sea rises, burying his sturdy prow in tremendous, tangled swells. Gaunt, spare rigging groans and sways, but weathered fibre holds. The sea has gone mad beneath him, threatening to scuttle her tormentor, but in the grip of loves great passion, the scarred little craft that is Artie holds to its course. With decks awash, beyond fear, beyond hope, in joyous manly thrust...On to the center of churning, spuming fury, on to the final climb, the great tidal wave of oblivion...the great fall at the end of the world.

The heavy laden air settles. The great body of the sea steams with calm and gentle swells. The pale and smiling moon glows from horizons pillow...and the little craft lists to port, riding humbly loves ample bosom and he sleeps.

Gerry Strong

A PUG NAMED CHARLOTTE

It all started when Charlotte put on a hooded sweater, stood on her hind legs, and followed some kids into school.

At first, when she got to the door, she was sent away. Then Charlotte saw a sweater on the ground. She had an idea. She wiggled into the sweater. It had a hood. She pulled it over her head.

There was something in a pocket: SUNGLASSES! She knew what they were. She put them on.

She got up on her hind legs. Now no one stopped her at the door.

She followed the boys and girls into a room. A lady talked a lot and made marks on a board. Charlotte watched and listened very politely. She tried to copy everything the boys and girls did.

After awhile, Charlotte began to act like them. And she discovered she could even talk to them.

Charlotte loved mysteries. She decided to become a detective and solve them.

She made a sign. She had business cards printed with her picture on them. She gave them to everyone she met.

She solved many crimes and mysteries. She became a very good detective.

Now she is hoping to solve the mystery of a whispering gold mine.

THE WHISPERING GOLD MINE
A Pug Detective Charlotte Mystery

"I see it," said five year old Timmy. He pointed to an old wooden sign.

"I see it too," said Penny.

The sign said: *Whispering Gold Mine.*

Pug Detective Charlotte saw it. She was in Colorado with her friends.

They had come to see a whispering gold mine.

"Do you think we'll hear it whisper?" asked Timmy.

Charlotte wanted to find out why an old gold mine would whisper.

"Do you think we'll dig for gold?" asked Timmy.

"I don't know," said Penny.

"That's what they do in a mine," said Timmy. "They dig for gold."

"Not all mines," said Penny. "They dig for other stuff too." She had that know-it-all look. Head up. Nose in the air.

"Yeah, I know," said Timmy. He was used to his sister. She was seven. Most times she was smarter.

They got closer to the sign. Charlotte saw cars parked near it.
And a lot of people.
Then a man said, "Welcome to the Whispering Gold Mine."
But Charlotte didn't see any gold mine.
Just the sign. And trees, grass, weeds.
And the high rocky mountain.
The man was tall. He wore jeans and a shirt. His boots looked
old and scuffed. On his head was a heavy-looking hat.
He waved his arm. "Follow me."
Then they walked right into the mountain!
"This is so exciting," said Penny.
The walls were dirt and rock. The air was cool. It felt damp.
Charlotte wrinkled her nose. She sniffed.
"It smells old and wet and dirty," she said.
Penny and Timmy knew Charlotte could talk. They remembered
how she had followed them into school. Then she had started to act
like them.
"A long time ago, men dug this mine in the mountain. They
were looking for gold," the guide said.

Charlotte thought the mine
looked like a cave. Only this cave
had lights. Lights on wires along
the ceiling,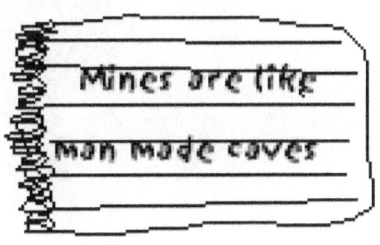

She wrote in her notebook.

The man pointed to the hat on his head.
"Rocks can fall. The miners wore hard-hats like this. You will
all have to wear one, too," he said.
A lot of hard-hats were lined up on a shelf. The man went over
to the shelf. He gave hats to Penny and Timmy.
Timmy put his hat on. "Now I'm a real miner," he said.
The man found a small hat for Charlotte.
The hard-hat was heavy. It wasn't made for a pug.
It hung over her eyes.

All Charlotte could see was the dirt floor.

And feet. Lots of feet.

Then there was a loud roaring and banging. Everyone turned toward the noise.

Carts came around a corner.

"Oh look," said Timmy. "Like a little railroad." He pointed to rails on the ground.

They followed the man. They got into the carts.

Clickity clack, clickity clack, went the metal wheels on the metal tracks. The carts rattled. The metal wheels squeaked.

They were going down. Down deep underground.

Deep into the old mine.

"Why do they call this the Whispering Gold Mine?" someone asked.

The man smiled. "There is a legend," he said. "It says miners heard whispering. They never found out who or what it was. Even today, people say they hear it."

"Do you think we will hear it whisper?" Timmy asked.

"Close your eyes. Be very quiet," the man said. "Maybe you will."

Charlotte closed her eyes. She listened very carefully.

Then she heard it! *The mine was whispering!*

But when she opened her eyes, she noticed it was just some people whispering.

They got out of the carts. The man pointed to the wall. Charlotte, Penny and Timmy went over to it.

Everyone crowded around. They saw small lines of something shiny.

"Is that the gold?" asked Timmy. "Those tiny little lines?"

The man nodded.

"It doesn't look like very much gold," said Penny.

"The line is called a vein. It goes deep into the wall. The miners take a pick. They dig all the gold out," said the man.

"Wow. Must take a long time," said Timmy.

They returned to the entrance in the carts. Timmy put their hard-hats on the shelf.

They were quiet as they left the mine.

"I didn't hear the mine whisper," said Penny. "Did you?"

Timmy and Charlotte shook their heads.

They started back to their cabin.

They hiked along a mountain stream.

That's when Charlotte fell in.

She was in trouble. Big trouble.

Water covered her head.

Cold, icy water. She tried hard to dog paddle.

She moved her little legs.

Hard and fast. Fast and hard.

Another wave washed over her. She was going to drown.

She was sure of it.

Now she would never see the old gold mine. She would never find out why it whispered.

She pushed her little pug nose up through the water.

She gulped for air.

"Help. Help," she yelped.

She felt a pull on her tail. And then she was free of the cold water. Penny let go of Charlotte. She looked down at her.

She asked, "What were you doing in the water?"

Charlotte felt foolish. She had been chasing a chipmunk. She had slipped off a rock. Right into the little mountain stream.

Charlotte shivered.

"Did you think the water would be warm? It's melted snow.

The streams carry it down from the top of the mountain," Penny said.

She took her jacket. She wiped Charlotte dry.

Charlotte didn't care about an old gold mine anymore. Even if it could whisper.

She was cold. She just wanted a warm blanket. And maybe a cup of hot chocolate.

* * *

Charlotte woke up.

Morning sun was shining in the cabin window. Timmy and Penny were outside sitting on a rock.

They were pouring cereal from a box into bowls.

Charlotte went out and joined them. They set a bowl down for her.

It was quiet on the mountain. Only the sound of crunch, crunch as they ate the cereal.

"We should go back," said Penny.

"What?" said Timmy.

"We should go back to the mine," said Penny. "Maybe it will whisper next time."

Charlotte thought about going back. Maybe there was still a chance to hear whispering. Maybe she could discover the mystery of the old mine.

They finished their cereal.

Charlotte took her backpack. It had her notebook. And doggie treats in case she got hungry.

They left the cabin. They started up the mountain path.

They hiked along the mountain stream.

This time, Charlotte didn't chase any chipmunks. She didn't want to fall in again.

Soon they were at the mine. They looked around.

"Where is everyone?" asked Timmy.

Penny went up to the door. She pulled on the handle. The door opened.

They looked at each other.

Charlotte peeked in the door.

"Hello," said Timmy.

"Hello," said Penny.

"Where is everyone?" asked Timmy again.

They walked into the dark mine. The only light was from the open door.

Penny took hard-hats off the shelf. They put them on.

They listened.

"I don't hear anything, do you?" asked Timmy.

Charlotte didn't hear anything. She thought they should leave. The mine was dark. They were alone. Maybe it wasn't safe.

"I'm scared," said Timmy.

"Shhh," said Penny. "Listen."

Now Timmy heard it. Charlotte heard it too. A kind of *wooooo* sound. High. Then low.

"It's whispering," said Penny.

Timmy moved closer to Charlotte. "Where is it coming from?" he asked.

Charlotte perked up her little black ears. She listened. She couldn't tell. It sounded like it was coming from everywhere.

And then, the whispering stopped.

They waited. All was quiet. Too quiet. Too dark.

"Run," said Timmy. He started to run. They all ran as fast as they could.

Back to the entrance. Timmy tossed their hard-hats on the shelf. They dashed out the door.

"Did you hear it?" asked Timmy.

Penny nodded. "I heard it," she said.

Charlotte had heard to too.

They returned to their cabin.

* * *

145

Timmy and Penny were in their PJ's.

They sat on Penny's bed.

Timmy hugged his stuffed bear. Penny hugged her knees.

"I heard whispering," she said.
"I know I did."

Timmy nodded. He was sure he had too. Charlotte was sure she had heard something.

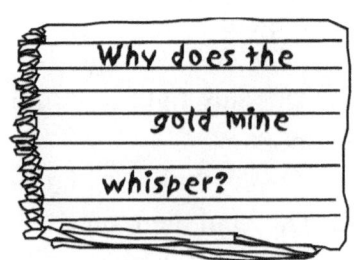

She wrote in her notebook.

"We have to find out why it whispers," Penny said.

Charlotte and Timmy looked at her.

Charlotte wanted to go back. She wanted to solve the mystery of the old gold mine.

"It was scary. What if something BIG is hiding in the dark?" asked Timmy.

"It wasn't scary when the people were there, was it?" asked Penny.

"No...," said Timmy.

"We just have to go back when everyone is there," said Penny.

"Yeah, that would be okay," said Timmy.

That sounded good to Charlotte too.

Penny crawled under her covers.

"Let's go tomorrow," she said.

Timmy nodded. He curled up in his bed.

Charlotte curled up next to Penny. Soon she was asleep.

* * *

In the morning when they woke up, the sun was bright on the mountain.

Aspen trees swayed in the breeze. Their white bark reflected the sunlight. Cool weather had turned their leaves gold.

The three explorers hiked up the mountain. This time, Timmy

was in the lead. Penny followed. Charlotte trotted along. Her short little legs took two steps to their one.

Then they were at the old mine again.

Timmy looked around. "I don't see a lot of cars."

"Maybe we are a little early," said Penny.

They walked over to the entrance. The old wooden door was open. Charlotte peeked in.

"Hello," called Timmy.

"Hello," came a voice back.

Lights came on. The lights that hung from the ceiling.

A man came into view.

"Who are you?" asked Penny.

"I work here. I keep things in good repair," he said.

"Why is no one at the mine?" asked Timmy.

"We are closing now. It's winter and there will be snow."

"We want to find out about the whispering," Penny said.

"That's a mystery that may never be solved. But you can come in," he said.

They went into the mine. Inside, he gave them the hard-hats to wear. They followed him. They listened.

"I guess the mine doesn't have anything to say today," Timmy said.

"The mine doesn't whisper all the time," the man said. "Sometimes you hear it. Sometimes, you don't."

Then Charlotte's little black ears perked up. She could hear it! The others could hear it too!

"Where is it coming from?" asked Timmy in a quiet voice.

"No one has been able to find out," said the man.

Charlotte walked around. She listened. She went closer to the rough rocky wall. She climbed up a rock. Then two.

She listened some more. She moved along the wall. She climbed a little higher.

She listened. The whispering was getting louder.

The wall was a little like the side of the mountain. Rocks stuck out. There were narrow ledges where Charlotte could walk.

And there were holes where she could poke her little head in.

She could feel cool air coming from one of these holes.

The sound was louder there. The hole was big enough for her to crawl into.

There the sound was very loud. But the hole had gotten narrow. And then the whispering had stopped.

She wiggled herself out.

She began to back up. Then the whispering started again.

She moved forward against the rocks. The whispering stopped!

Moving back, it started!

Moving forward it stopped!

Charlotte's fur began to rise. It always did that when she was close to solving a crime or mystery. And she was sure she had solved this mystery!

She backed up and turned around. She ran down to the bottom.

Timmy grabbed her. He hugged her.

"You're all right!" he said. He put her down.

"We heard the whispering stop. Then start," said Penny.

Charlotte nodded. She had a big smile on her face.

Penny saw Charlotte's smile.

"I think Charlotte has solved the mystery of the old mine," said Penny.

Charlotte stretched up tall. "Wind comes through holes between the rocks," she said.

"So, that's what makes the whispering sound," Penny said. "It's because of the wind!"

"Boy, you're smart, Charlotte," said Timmy.

They went over to the man.

Timmy pointed to Charlotte.

"Charlotte solved the mystery of the whispering," he said proudly.

"Yeah," said Penny. "She found a narrow hole where air was coming in from outside."

"Well," said the guide, "Charlotte is a very smart dog."

Penny hugged Charlotte. "You're a great detective," she said.

"Yeah, she solved the mystery," said Timmy.

It was so simple—just the wind between the rocks!

Charlotte felt good about solving the mystery. Now whenever she heard the wind, it would always remind her of the whispering of the old gold mine.

CHARLOTTE'S NOTES

The Pike's Peak Gold Rush (later known as the Colorado Gold Rush) was the boom in gold prospecting and mining in the Pike's Peak Country of western Kansas Territory and southwestern Nebraska Territory of the United States that began in July 1858 and lasted until roughly the creation of the Colorado Territory on February 28, 1861. An estimated 100,000 gold seekers took part in one of the greatest gold rushes in North American history. The participants in the gold rush were known as Fifty-Niners after 1859, the peak year of the rush and often used the motto *Pike's Peak or Bust!* (wikipedia)

J. E. Michals

A VENUS FLIGHT TRAP

Commodore Cock Roach—not his precise Venusian nomenclature, but a close enough Earth English approximation—was ecstatic. That was not his precise emotion, but once again, a reasonable approximation.

The *Ultimate, Beneficent Planetary Nest and Garbage Heap* was the sole surviving roach colony on Venus—after 1,893,782 generations of Inter-Cockroach Civil War. And the colony had finally organized and launched its *First Off-Planet Military Expedition of Unbridled Conquest.*

And he, Cock, was the *Head Roach* of this exceptional expedition. How much more glory could attach to a life that lasted only 0.56 solar transitions? (No need to answer that; it's a rhetorical question.)

In all, it had taken almost 1.1 million Venusian Cockroach (VCR for short) generations to invent things like Space Flight and Indoor Outhouses. It took that long because although VCRs were bigger and longer-lived compared to their Earth-bound counterparts, VCRs didn't always fly with a full set of wings.

Nonetheless, the VCRs had learned enough to build an invasion fleet and blasted it into an equatorial orbit. The expedition then slingshotted out—using a gravity boost from the Sun—toward Earth. Mercury was closer, but Earth looked nicer.

The fleet used two revolutions around their planet to start the slingshot maneuver because The Maximum Roach's favored expression was: *"You can chirp that two times!"* That expression came from…

well, never mind. That's a different type of tangent, and we don't have time to go there right now. Maybe in some other story.

Anyhow, the invasion fleet was on its way.

***

Lunar-based *Meteor Automated Defense System* (MADS for short) No. 13—an unlucky number in both Earth and Venusian cultures —detected and began tracking the incoming swarm of hippo-sized *VCR Planetary Assault Pods* (V-PAPs for short) as they approached Earth.

MADS did not enumerate individual Pods. If it had, it would have tallied 7,777,777—seven being considered a propitious number in VCR culture. MADS simply observed that an immense swarm of what appeared to be modest-sized meteors was on a collision course with the home planet.

No. 13 was an old station, due for a major software upgrade Real Soon Now. But as was typical of such Halliburton Space Corporation projects, the money for the contract was in company coffers busy collecting interest, while the actual engineering work was delayed by ... who knows what.

That, in any case, is why No. 13's software did not consider the unusual nature of the incoming meteor swarm—such as the fact that meteors do not decelerate on a non-linear basis when entering a gravity well.

This was perhaps a fortuitous error for Earthlings. Or maybe it affected the outcome not at all. Hard to say.

Either way, the VCRs would have considered MADS No. 13 a ball-buster—if they had known it existed, and if they had balls in the anatomical sense.

But they didn't know about MADS, and even if they had....

The target-acquisition-and-analysis computer of No. 13 took its good old time—as computer systems measure time—considering the problem. It invested nearly one full second on data processing and decision-tree dissection before calculating a final firing solution.

If MADS No. 13 was a trifle slow computationally, once it completed its cogitations it was digitally decisive. It launched 16 (not an especially significant number in either Earth or Venusian cultures) *Nano-Nucleotidic, Multi-Mosaic, Proton-Prohibitive, Quasi-Quarkish, Absolute-Annihilator* rockets. Nine dispersive warheads per rocket. Humanity's very best.

The rest—as they say on both Earth and Venus—is history.

VCR designers never considered that the planet Earth—and specifically its dominant life form thereon—might not care to be overrun by Venusian Cockroaches. Therefore the VCRs had not equipped their fleet with either long-range sensors or defensive shields. (VCRs were not overly intellectual, and had both a figurative and literal tendency to get their antennas tangled.)

The MADS-initiated rockets—their warheads disbursed in a dynamic-hexagon defensive array—intercepted the incoming V-PADS almost before the roaches realized their pending doom. Only one scout ship had time to semaphore back to the trailing fleet a brief, partial message.

That transmission—which gains nuances in translation from VCR to Earth English—was approximately: *"Oh Great Cock, we are about to take it up the...."*

Message Ends.

RESCUE

Heat lightning flashed over nearby mountains. It reminded the old man of unexpected events that occur in life. "Had too many of those lately," he muttered aloud to his shadow as it slithered ahead of him on the asphalt.

Joseph Wolfe was walking back from an unplanned grocery-shopping trip. A quarter mile behind him was a scruffy town with a name he had not bothered to learn. A quarter mile ahead was his motorhome, set up for an overnight camp in a shallow arroyo.

At the edge of an abandoned gas station parking lot stood the town's last streetlight—a skinny sentinel faced off against darkness. Joseph was a hundred yards beyond this outrider of civilization when he heard the cry.

It wasn't a scream, or a shout for help. It was an involuntary outburst of pain. A predator had found prey.

Curiosity kills a lot of things, Joseph reminded himself. Nonetheless, he halted, turned around, leaned on his oak hiking stick, squinted into the night's obscurity.

Nothing. No sound, no shifting shapes, no running feet.

And then, there was.

"Get her!" a male voice ordered. "Little bitch stabbed me."

Dangerous prey; it fights back.

A small, slender figure moved into the weak circle of light that helped to define the front of the station. Three larger figures maneuvered around her, cutting off her escape to the street, herding her toward the shadowed side of the vacant building.

The smaller figure lashed out each time one of the bigger ones lunged at her. That one would leap back out of range, while the other two used the distraction to maneuver closer, seeking an advantage.

"Matter of time," Joseph said aloud. "And not much." *Last time I saw something like this I was too cowardly to intervene.*

The old man closed his eyes, breathed deep and slow, envisioned an outcome. He opened his eyes just as the foursome, still doing their strange ballet, disappeared behind the far side of the gas station.

He shrugged off his backpack, dropped it to the ground, bent over, pulled items from it.

I spent decades studying martial arts in case I ever had an opportunity to redeem myself. Time to find out how well I learned.

Joseph clipped a high-intensity Sure-Fire flashlight onto the right rear pocket of his cargo pants, slipped a small canister of pepper spray into his left-leg pocket. He hefted a 15-ounce can of lima beans in his hand, testing the weight, giving it a few practice swings—as if preparing to throw a heavy baseball. He dropped the can into his right-leg pocket.

He picked up his staff in his left hand and stood. The old man smiled in the direction of the chase scene, then announced to the night: "Time for an old wolf to march into the lions' den. And eat the lions."

****

"You shouldda left town sooner," a male voice—arrogant, condescending. "You mightta got away. But it was easy to trail you when it got dark, without nobody, not even you, seein' us."

Joseph slowed; his heart rate was elevated, but not significantly. He'd done a modified version of the airborne shuffle—a technique he'd learned almost 50 years ago at Fort Benning—to cover the distance from his abandoned backpack to the front of the gas station.

"Hangin' round the dumpster behind the Pizza Palace was a bad idea." A different male voice, also disdainful. "Tells us what you are—a trash picker. Somebody nobody's gonna miss."

157

As Joseph listened, he considered dropping to the ground so he could peer around the corner of the gas station from a low vantage point. He decided against it. Probably the predators were having too much fun baiting their victim to notice him. But there was too much tactical disadvantage if one of them was alert; he might attack before Joseph could scramble to his feet and counter.

"We find us some good huntin' by watchin' that bin." The voice of No. 2 continued. "Mostly old men, bums, we can chase down and beat on. But you, pretty thing, you are prime meat."

The prey, a teenage girl, was backed up against a graffiti-covered wall. Whatever weapon she had been using to fend off her assailants was now gone. At least it wasn't in her hands, which, Joseph noticed, were balled into fists, ready to jab out at whoever closed with her first.

The area between Joseph and the foursome was an oily wasteland—the consequence of decades of chemical dumpings by station users. A clutter of abandoned mechanical parts littered the ground as far as the old man could see in the dim light of the quarter moon.

Joseph pulled the can of beans from his pocket, juggled it a few times in his hand, then stepped around the corner.

He moved with care, wanting to get as close as possible before the predators became aware of his presence. He was a dozen feet away when one of the trio demanded, "Hey, who the hell's this?"

Joseph assumed a hunched pose, leaned on his staff, waved his can in the air.

He said in a slurred voice, "You fellash got a can open'r? Got a can uff stuff here and can't get 'er open. An' I'm hungry."

"Gimme that, old man." The voice of No. 2—a modest-sized, greasy-haired, 20-something. He was dressed in dirty, denim coveralls and a plaid, long-sleeve shirt. "I'll open it for you. I'll bust it over your head."

Laughter from his companions. Joseph smiled, as if he too enjoyed the joke.

The man stepped toward Joseph.

"Giff it to you, Young Feller? If you shay sho." Joseph's arm swung in a circle—down, around, up, forward. From a distance of about eight feet, he hurled the can at his antagonist. Caught off guard, the man staggered as the projectile drove edge-first into his chest.

Joseph allowed the momentum of his throw to carry him forward. As he moved, his right hand grasped the midpoint of his staff. Now only a few feet from his opponent, Joseph thrust the stick—tip first—to spear the man in the solar plexus. The force of the strike drove the man backward.

As a finishing blow, Joseph moved both hands to the handle of his staff and whirled it overhead, angled downward like a slashing sword. It crunched into the vagus nerve on the left side of the man's neck. He crumpled.

Went down like he was pole axed.

Joseph allowed himself an inner smile as he stepped over the inert body to engage his next-closest opponent.

The old man swung his staff like a scythe—both hands near the handle to provide maximum leverage. The second man—bigger than the first and no longer in the grip of surprise—anticipated a blow to the head. He threw up his arms in defense.

Think you can grab my stick? Guess again.

Joseph bent forward and swept in low with the staff. The tip struck the side of the hoodlum's left knee. The joint collapsed. The man screeched as his leg buckled.

Joseph once again changed hand position on the staff as he rose up to full height. He spun the stick in a 180-degree vertical arc that ended at the back of the man's head.

Two down.

The third man seized the girl in a chokehold from behind. "Back off, man, or I kill the broad."

That would spoil my whole evening.

Joseph shrugged. "Nothing to me, Bud. I never saw her before in my life." He edged toward the pair. "I'm just here to have some fun of my own."

Misunderstanding Joseph's meaning, Mr. Stranglehold said, "Whaddayah mean? You want this piece of ass for yourself?"

Joseph continued to close. "In a manner of speaking. Let's negotiate." He tossed down his stick. "See, a gesture of my good will."

The assailant smiled, heaved the girl aside. "You made a mistake, givin' up your weapon, old man." The would-be killer charged Joseph, flicking open a folding knife as he came.

Rather than retreat, Joseph moved forward. His high-intensity combat flashlight now in his right hand, his pepper-spray canister in his left. Joseph clicked on the light; the brilliant, focused beam overloaded the other man's optic nerves.

Joseph's attacker closed his eyes, crossed both arms in front of his face, skidded to a stop. Joseph delivered a classic, step-behind side-kick. His boot heel smashed into the man's stomach. The man doubled over, reflexively dropping his hands.

Joseph thrust out his left arm and drenched his opponent's face with pepper spray. The man gave a choked scream, dropped to his knees, and began rubbing desperately at his eyes.

Joseph pivoted and drove a hard round-house kick into the side of the man's head.

The girl had scuttled away during this final skirmish. When Joseph turned toward her, she was partly hidden behind a decaying wooden box. The old man waved his flashlight in the direction of the street.

"We should go."

He bent to recover his hiking stick.

"Don't touch me!"

The girl huddled in upon herself, thin, bare arms wrapped around jeans-clad legs.

She looks as fragile as a porcelain figurine.

"I won't hurt you; I promise."

Something moved in the darkness. Joseph stood and swept his light around to survey the area. The first man he had put down was trying to rise. The man groaned once, fell backward, made no second attempt.

"What are you going to do?" the girl asked.

"About what?"

Joseph found and retrieved his can of beans.

"Them." The girl lifted her left arm off her legs and waved her hand in an arc to indicate the immobile trio.

Joseph clicked off his light.

"Nothing. I was never here, so I can't do anything about them."

"You just crushed all three of them. How can you say you.... Oh!"

Quick to catch on; good survival skill.

"In a few hours I'll be down the road and invisible," Joseph said. "You'd best be gone too."

He moved away toward the road.

"Go where?"

Something I hadn't considered.

"Wherever you came from, I guess," Joseph called over his shoulder. He progressed two steps further, but turned around when the girl sniffled.

"I can't go back where I came from. I came from nowhere."

The voice drifted out of the darkness, the girl unseeable in the deep shadows.

Joseph hissed out a breath. He clicked on his flashlight and swept the beam over the girl, giving her substance once again.

"Can you walk?"

The girl twisted her head away, used a hand to cover her eyes.

"Yes. They didn't hurt me." A pause. "Much."

The old man ingested a slow, deep breath as he thought through possible scenarios.

Wonder how long she's had to survive on her own.

"I have a vehicle down the road. If you can walk there, I'll take you." Another deep breathe. "To the next town."

The girl inched her way upward, using the wall for support. "I need my stuff. It's all I've got."

"How much stuff? Where?"

The girl gestured.

"Around the other side, where they jumped me."

Joseph stiffened. He rescanned the area with his light. Nothing had changed, but he remained wary.

"You're sure you can walk?" He watched as the girl took a few

161

tentative steps.

"Yeah. I'm okay." The girl brushed herself; stood straighter.

"Take only what you can carry easily." Joseph pointed in the direction of his campsite. "That way. Half mile up the road."

He waited for a response. None was forthcoming.

"Ten minutes," Joseph said. "No more." He strode away at a brisk pace.

The girl hesitated, then followed the old man—from darkness into the light.

ROADSIDE CONVERSATION

"Drop it or I'll kill her!" he shouts again.

Redundant, flashes through my mind. Stupid thought, but…

"No," I respond. "I don't think so." I ease backward two steps.

Keep him talking; keep him off balance. That thought could be a comment to either of us, but it's just one part of my mind talking to another.

"What do you mean, "NO!" His voice rises in both pitch and volume.

He's nervous, which makes him less stable, which makes him more dangerous.

"Drop the gun or I'll blow her fuckin' head off!"

"Then what?" I ask.

I'm reminded of a famous general's quote: "Be polite; be professional; have a plan to kill everyone you meet."

My voice and my movements are casual, gradual, unruffled. Time slows, as my speed of thought increases.

When Punko wedged his pistol against Jill's temple, he didn't so much gain leverage as begin a countdown toward death. Threatening my wife is a peculiar form of suicide.

"What do you mean, 'Then what?' Then she's fucking dead…."

Instead of commenting, I take another step backward.

"What the fuck are you doin', man? Stand still!"

I stay still. And silent. For a moment. Then I begin weaving my lie. "We can work this out," I say. *You let go of her; I kill you. Straight-forward. Something for each of us.*

"I ain't shittin' you man! You put the gun down or I'll kill her now!" *Even a bad Hollywood screenwriter would have trouble believing this dialog.*

My breathing continues slow and deep.

"Then what?" I repeat.

He's not a quick study. No surprise—dumb and dangerous often go together.

I take another step backward. Every move is cautious. I don't want to spook the prey. I also don't want to disrupt my aim. His right eye is a looming target—clear in the tactical scope atop my .22-caliber carbine.

Not much punch, but accurate. And lots more rounds than his pistol. Only takes one. Too bad it works both ways.

I can kill him anytime I choose. When a killer meets a killer.... He apparently doesn't comprehend that. Killing him is not the problem. Killing him cleanly with a .22, that is the problem. *Even if I put the first one through his eye, his reflexes might squeeze the trigger.*

Jill winces and makes a small noise of pain as Punko twists the muzzle into the side of her head.

How do I get that pistol pointed away from Jill? Make a mistake; point your weapon at me instead of her.

"I want your car," he says. *And my life, too? And my pretty wife, as a bonus?*

I say nothing. I take another sliding step backward. By now I'm more than 10 meters from Jill and her captor. *Why captor? Why not "the punk with the gun". Whatever. Semantics some other time.*

The distance is not yet optimal, but every centimeter of separation helps me more than it helps him. My rifle is accurate over a greater distance than his pistol. Few people are good pistol shots. It takes a steady hand and lots of practice. *But he might get off a lucky shot.*

A scene from a Clint Eastwood spaghetti-Western flashes through my mind: *"When a man with a rifle meets a man with a pistol..."*

Pistol guy won the movie shootout. But this isn't a movie. And this no-name gunman isn't wearing body armor. And I'm not aiming for his body.

"You don't look stupid or suicidal," I say. Soft—but it carries well; there are no competing sounds. This strip of asphalt spearing through the scrub desert is soothingly quiet.

What to do after I kill him? Go to the police and explain what happened? That could get complicated. Maybe just bury the body and move on? I've done that before.

"Suicidal? What the fuck's that supposed to mean?" he demands.

Ah! Finally signs of intelligence. Diminished, but....

"I don't want you to kill her. I don't want to kill you. So let's make a deal...."

What about his motorcycle? Drive it away myself? Dump it a couple kilometers down the road? Maybe set fire to it to draw attention away from the burial site?

"You have the advantage," I say. "You're a killer—and I'm not." *Liar. Liar.* "But if you kill her, I'll kill you."

Oh, will I ever....

Another step back. To my surprise, Punko does the same, pulling Jill off balance. Her hands tug on his sleeve.

Shoot now! He's moving. He's off balance.

"I said stand still, man!" Punko shouts.

Too risky. Patience. A clean shot will come; it always does.

"Sure, whatever you say," I respond. "Let's talk this out." *Just a casual, roadside conversation.*

Does the hood of a car make a good shooting rest? Is kneeling a better shooting position than standing? Any thoughts about the shock characteristics of a .22 hollowpoint?

Jill is looking in my direction but not seeing me. She's not injured, but she also is not in the here-and-now. Ah, my love—*you lack experience in violent enterprises. I understand. No matter, I have enough experience for all three of us.*

"You let her go, you take the car and split. We won't try to stop you." *As Yoda said, there is no trying...*

"Give me the keys." *How about I give you a lead headache instead?*

"Okay. Let loose of her, we both lower our guns, I give you the keys...."

Too bad they're still in the car. Good thing you don't know that.

"The keys! Now!"

His arm tightens, cutting off Jill's air supply. Her fingernails dig into his arm.

Don't give him an edge, but give him something.

"I'll sweeten the deal. There's cash hidden in the car."

Don't spook him. Kill him, but don't spook him.

"Where?"

Good boy; get greedy; lose concentration.

"Underneath—a package wedged between the gas tank and the trunk."

Oh, my—the lies I tell. But in a good cause!

"G'me the keys and I'll let her go."

Go for his gun? How many snap shots can I get into his hand, his arm? Once again, risky, but....

"You need to let her go first. Then you can have it all." *The whole magazine. I'm generous; I'll even reload.*

"Yeah, right. You think I'm fuckin' stupid?"

I do. Then again, we all are. It's a matter of degree....

"I'm hoping you're smart. Smart enough to think this thing through, so we can make a deal." *Such a deal I have for you....*

The rifle seems weightless in my hands—though it's about eight pounds with scope and fully-loaded banana clip. Jill isn't a heavy weight either. *Would she seem heavier as dead weight?*

I easily maintain a steady sight picture. Despite the heat, I'm hardly perspiring.

Shoot out a knee? Right one is in sight, between her legs. Might work. The movement might draw his aim toward me. Then again, it might not.

"Suppose I give you the keys, then what?"

If Jill would just make a move, drop out of the way....

"You throw me the keys and we'll talk some more. I'm getting tired of this bullshit, man!" *Well, now, aren't we all.*

"All right," I say. *One of us has to show some good faith. Time is against us. All of us. Eventually another car is going to come along....*

"The keys are in the car. In the ignition."

Another step, this time to the side. *Pay attention now, Punko; this might be complex for you.*

"I'm going to step aside. Slowly. So you can check for yourself," I say. *Give me an opening; I'm ready.*

As I move, the gunman forces Jill forward. I shift again. No improvement; the gunman continues to keep Jill in front of him.

How many rounds to flatten a tire? Two tires, to be sure of halting him?

I sidle backward, three steps for two of his.

Come back on line, Jill. Look at me. Give me a sign.

The driver-side door to the car stands open. Jill was in a hurry to get to the figure sprawled on the roadway.

***

I'd been dozing when she braked.

"Motorcycle down, looks like a crash," she'd said.

I was slow coming awake; she dash out as I unbelted.

Bike looked okay; no skid marks, I'd thought. How'd he crash? Did he crash?

The "victim" had jumped up and seized Jill as she approached him.

She's naïve—and good hearted. Too bad she was driving. Too bad I was asleep.

Her abbreviated scream had mainlined adrenaline into me. I'd come fully alert—moments too late. Belatedly, I'd snatched the carbine and clip from under the blanket on the backseat. As I rolled out of the car, I'd loaded the rifle and come up in firing position—on target. More reflex than conscious thought.

***

Debrief later. Keep Punko in your sights. Be ready.

As the gunman pulls my wife around the car door, he removes his arm from her throat and grabs a handful of her hair. Jill is forced to half stand, half squat as the gunman leans to look into the car.

Is his gun loaded? What if he's empty and this is all a bluff? Forget "what if." Stay focused.

Punko manages to keep Jill in place as a shield. Points for him. Bullets next. He has to make a choice now: let Jill go—with or without a bullet—or try to drag her into the car. *Here's your chance, Punko; do the right thing.*

"Now you know I told you the truth," I say. "Let her go."

Shred just one tire. We'll need the car. One spare, one tire. Four or five rounds should suffice.

The gunman slides into the driver's seat; I hear the engine start. Death minus six seconds—and counting.

"Let her go!" Forceful this time. Power of suggestion. *Will it work?*

Jill starts to rise. *He gave up control of her to take control of the car.* She still blocks my view of the gunman.

The door slams shut. The sound doesn't surprise me; I don't mistake it for a gunshot.

The engine races. *What if she moves, but isn't fast enough? How far to a hospital? Where is a hospital?*

I wait for the chirp of tires. I wait for a clear shot. *"Ready on the left. Ready on the right. Ready on the firing line."*

While the gunman is distracted, I drop into prone shooting position. *You have one survival move, Punko—put it into* Drive *and floor it.*

Of course he could shoot Jill, then try for me. But I believe he has other plans. If he can kill me, he can do whatever he wants to with my wife; she isn't going anywhere. *He probably thinks he's got it all figured out. Don't we all?*

The driver-side window grinds down. *I was hoping I wouldn't hear that.* He pokes his pistol out, aimed slightly backward. I see a flash of it in the rear-view mirror.

Being left-handed gives him a shooting advantage in this situa-

168

tion. But the backup lights telegraph his intention.

It won't work, Punko; I've been ahead of you all along. Okay, not quite. Not for the first few seconds—but you had a head start.

The car rolls backward.

As the gunman's head clears Jill—who remains frozen in the roadway—I'm already on target. There's a look of surprise on Punko's face when he realizes I'm not where he expected me to be.

Commence firing.

Crosshairs settle onto his face, track his left eye, bounce when the rifle discharges.

I squeeze off three quick shots: "Ca-chunk; Ca-chunk; Ca-chunk." *You should have made a run for it, Punko; I might have let you go.*

Hollow-point, long-rifle bullets do not explode the braincase like high-powered projectiles would. The 40-grain pellets just punch in, then churn around—causing chaos. *Gives new meaning to the term: "Mush for brains...."*

The car continues to roll backwards, so I shoot out the left-front tire.The front end swings outward, the car glides into soft sand, the engine stalls.

Jill first, then the car, then....

As I jump up, I see another moving vehicle. *Can't be sure how far away it is; distance is deceptive in the clear, desert air.*

I sling the rifle over my shoulder, run to Jill, hold her, stroke her hair. As the vehicle comes closer, sunlight glints off a lightbar on the roof. *Highway Patrol.*

"Jill, wake up!" I give her a shake. "I'll be right back." I push away from her and dash to our car. I reach through the open window for the keys. The gunman is no hindrance; he's sprawled across the console and down into the passenger's footwell.

"Clutching his gun in his cold, dead hand...." Okay, technically his hand isn't cold. Yet.

I hurry to unlock the trunk, rummage out the spare tire.

The patrol car rolls to a stop several meters away, A pot-bellied trooper slowly climbs out, dons his hat, looks at Jill, straightens his posture and his shirt.

Another man with a pistol, interested in my wife.

I tuck the rifle beneath some luggage and slam the trunk closed.

He won't start out threatening Jill, so I won't need a firearm to deal with him—one way or another.

Peter Cruikshank

JULIA THE DREAMER

The silver dragon was barely visible in the overcast, predawn sky of Julia's dream. She had seen this particular beast before. Her dream-view shifted from the ground to the air and she looked down on the dragon and its rider, a man cloaked in armor to match the dragon's scales. Julia had only watched the silver-armored man from a distance, but for some reason was drawn to him. Previously she'd only seen him in full helm. Now, with his helmet removed, long golden hair floated behind him.

Movement caught her eye. Four giant hawks rose from the clouds. In the past, Julia had only observed the hawks on the horizon. They were a more recent addition to her dreams, but she knew they were at odds with the dragon riders.

Whack! The loud sound made her jerk upright at her desk. "Watch out for the hawks!" she called. Julia was rewarded with laughter. Her cheeks warmed as her classmates continued to enjoy her humiliation.

"Ms. Julia Johnson!"

She turned to face Ms. Matheson. The teacher impatiently tapped a ruler against her palm, the same ruler that had often awakened Julia before when the teacher used it to strike her desk.

"I'm sorry, Ms. Matheson." Julia shook her head, still caught between reality and her daydream.

"What hawks?" the teacher demanded, her frown deepening.

Julia hesitated; the images of the dragon and birds faded.

"Ms. Johnson!"

"There aren't any hawks. I'm sorry, I was just daydreaming."

"This is the third time in two weeks." Ms. Matheson pulled her shoulders back and, though Julia thought it impossible, the elderly woman stiffened her posture even more.

"I'm sorry."

Ms. Matheson evidently expected more, but after a long moment of silence, she stomped back to her desk. As the irate teacher fumbled through some papers, picked several up, then spun and marched back to Julia, Ms. Matheson's face turned the color of strawberry Kool-Aid.

"Well, little Ms. Dreamer," her voice rose with each word. "Maybe you can stay awake long enough in detention to complete these." The teacher dropped the advanced calculus problems onto Julia's desk before returning to the front of the room.

Julia managed to keep a smile from her lips. *She's probably forgotten I already have detention today.*

She would have to get a couple of the problems wrong. Otherwise she would infuriate the grouchy old teacher even more. It was the same in every class. As soon as she saw a problem or was asked a question—in History, English, or any other subject—Julia somehow knew the answer. She had asked about this and the other strange things that had happened since she had passed into womanhood, but her aunt would only grumble something about Julia's mother under her breath.

Julia walked sluggishly down the long lane to her aunt's shabby farmhouse, nearly a mile off the busy Texas highway. She could taste the dust blown off the old road and nearby fields. It was drier than normal for winter—as if the rain gods had overlooked them—again. At least the High School Principal, Mr. Randall, had been kind to her that afternoon. He had only shaken his head as he read the slip Ms. Matheson had sent with her. He warned her to improve her attitude in that 'as-a-father-and-educator-I-know-best' tone, but did not add more days to her detention.

Julia stamped her shoes on the steps and then pulled open the squeaky screen. She placed her hand on the split wood and cracked paint of the weather-worn door. Julia took a deep breath as she pushed it open and entered the drab front room. Everything was either a faded grey or baby-poop brownish-green.

"Is that you, Julia?" her aunt called from the kitchen in her familiar biting tone.

Julia thought of several sharp remarks, but responded in as pleasant a voice as she could muster—the consequences of not doing so wasn't worth the moment of rebellion. "Yes, it's me."

"The teacher keep you after again?"

Julia could feel the sarcasm from the other room. For the millionth time she wondered how this elderly woman could be her father's sister. Not biological, as her aunt often reminded her. She knew little of her father other than he had been adopted when Julia's grandmother remarried more than eighteen years after Julia's aunt had been born.

"Yes."

"Daydreaming again?"

"Yes."

"Dreamer. Nothing but a dreamer."

Julia could easily imagine her aunt's head shaking just like Mr. Randall's.

"Julia the Dreamer." Her aunt's voice trailed off with additional disparaging comments about Julia's parents. This always happened when she got in trouble, or did something odd.

Julia started up the stairs to her room, but a harsh command came from the kitchen, "Get to your chores. Supper will be ready soon. I want you in bed early. Maybe then you'll quit disrespecting your teachers."

After the grim diagnosis this past summer, her aunt's manner had grown even harsher, but Julia couldn't really blame her. Heart disease wasn't something anyone wanted to hear. Her aunt had already declared that the day after Julia left for college, the farm was going up for sale.

Julia didn't want to make life any harder for her aunt. Her voice became as respectful as she could summon, "Yes, Ma'am."

She put her books on the stairs and headed out to the barn. Between detention, chores, and supper, she wouldn't finish until after dusk. Then it would be off to her room for the rest of the evening. *Only a few more months.*

Moonlight filtered in through stained lace curtains and broken shutters. It lit Julia's face as she lay awake in bed. The taste of the overcooked chicken from supper still stuck in her throat. *Is everything in Texas bone-dry?*

Like most nights, she comforted herself with thoughts of her parents. Not that she really remembered them—just images of a life that flashed into her mind. A time before she came to live with her aunt. *I wonder what they were like?* As much as she tried her efforts were sometimes followed by the same frustrated thought. *Why would they leave me with her?* This brought on a little bitterness that she quickly dampened with rationalization. *They had their reasons.*

Lately, Julia had been reluctant to fall asleep. The dreams had come more frequently over the last few months…and had become darker. Not the same exact dream—more like a series of dreams, as if she were watching a TV series. They had begun two days after her first period which led to monthly dreams for the first year that matched her menstrual cycle. Then twice a month, increasing to weekly until now—five years later—in her last year of high school, they came almost every night and even in the middle of the day.

The dreams involved a castle and surrounding lands. People dressed in antiquated clothing. Some of the men wore swords. The early dreams were of celebrations and outings into the countryside. Unlike her, the people seemed happy.

And dragons! A few were always around the castle in an area set aside to house them, while others were free to travel to and from nearby mountains. Over the last month giant hawks—a third the size of the dragons—had attacked travelers on the road and could be seen from the castle, though at a great distance.

Of late, Julia's dreams had centered on the silver dragon and its rider, more so than any others in the castle. It was as if she was being called—pulled toward them. The more Julia focused the wearier she became. After a wide yawn, her eyelids lowered slowly. She fought against sleep, but her breath became deeper as her thoughts faded away.

The murkiness of sleep lifted and the dream filled her thoughts again.

Julia found herself far from the castle. She looked up into an overcast dawn sky as morning broke over the forested foothills. It was the same sky as in the classroom daydream. The silver dragon dropped through the bottom of the clouds, twisting in the air to avoid the four hawks that attacked it.

In her dreams Julia had only seen the massive hawks at a distance. She had not realized that men rode upon them. At least she thought they were men—they were still far away, but were coming closer as the silver dragon dove toward the ground.

Two of the hawks plunged toward the dragon's back, while the other two approached from below, flying just above the tree tops.

Using the claws on its wings, the dragon easily fended off the two flying creatures attacking from underneath.

Julia realized the lower hawks were simply a diversion.

The first of the diving hawks came at the silver-armored rider with its talons spread. As it plummeted toward the dragon, a long lance held by the hawk's rider was thrust forward. If the spear didn't pierce the dragon rider; the hawk's talons would tear him apart.

She was surprised when the man rose to stand on the dragon's back. His hair whipped in the wind as he drew a long sword from over his back. The blade flashed and sizzled like a bolt of lightning as he held it over his head with both hands.

A heartbeat before the lance reached him, he leapt. While he rose more than fifteen feet into the air, he swung his sword down and then back up in an arc. The blade cleanly severed the tip of the lance as he soared another half-dozen feet past the hawk. The man twisted. The movement brought the sword around with increased speed. When it struck the hawk's rider it sliced completely through his shoulder.

The silver dragon beat back the lower attackers and flipped over to strike out at the hawk as the dead rider fell from the hawk's saddle. The dragon's claws ripped through the attacking bird's neck, spewing blood across the brightening sky to fall like rain on the trees below.

Julia wanted to cheer, though she knew nothing of the dragon or its rider.

Her elation was short-lived as the second diving hawk attacked. The man tried to twist out of its path, but a talon swept across to bat the rider up and away. His blade flew through the air ahead of him.

The dragon flipped again and sped after its rider. The hawk shot past and had to veer abruptly to avoid colliding with the tall trees.

The silver-armored man fell. His body flopped about, buffeted by the wind. He appeared to be unconscious—or worse.

The dragon swooped down toward the sword.

The dragon had four thick legs with clawed paws, but also running along the front of the wings were what appeared to be arms. At the end of each of these limbs was a thumb-like appendage and four long talons.

It seized the weapon with the talons protruding from the end of the wing. It then grasped its rider with a rear claw before the man crashed into the tree tops.

For a short distance it rose just above the forest canopy then dropped down and disappeared from Julia's view. A moment later it rose again and winged steadily toward the distant mountains with the captured sword easily visible. The three remaining hawks gave futile chase, unable to match the dragon's speed.

Light struck through Julia's closed eyelids.

She threw a hand up to block the sunlight pouring into her room through the broken slats in the blinds. Her heart beat rapidly and she took several deep breathes to calm herself.

The Dream.

Julia sighed and shifted her weight to a shadowed spot on her bed. She lay there for a few moments, then exhaled in what sounded almost like a moan. *Another day on the farm.* The thought made her sad, deepening her already dour mood.

Somewhere in her memory, impressions of happier times lingered. Reds, blues, greens, and yellows colored every view. The sound of laughter accompanied an image of a man and a woman. Their faces were blurred, but she somehow knew they were beautiful. Normally they dressed in flowing robes, but sometimes they both wore armor of gold. The man had shoulder-length blond hair, and the woman had fiery ginger locks that draped over her shoulders and fell to her waist—hair a little longer than Julia's, but the color was the same. The vision always faded as quickly as it came, leaving Julia hungering for more.

I wonder.

The idea that they might be her parents excited her, even as it brought back the feelings of desertion that she tried not to focus on.

"Julia!" her aunt's voice rose up the stairs like a murky mist. "Your chores won't do themselves."

Julia shook her arms and legs the same way a dog flings off water. She dressed and went downstairs to eat a quick breakfast. It was Saturday, so no school, but this didn't mean Julia had the day off. Her aunt declared Julia was to go to the store after her morning chores, with more tasks for her when she returned. Julia only nodded, grabbed a heavy coat hung by the back door, fetched an empty basket from the pantry and headed out to the field to pick some of the late-ripening berries.

The sun hadn't been up long and dew still sat like small, glittering diamonds upon the high grass. As she trudged toward the field and the bushes on the other side, her jeans became damp halfway up her calves.

She put the large basket on the ground and started to pluck the berries, occasionally popping one into her mouth. The fruit's tartness was a nice change from her aunt's bland cooking and she enjoyed the way they burst, flooding her mouth with flavor when she bit into them.

Berry-picking was a mindless task and she gazed behind her at the farm and the flat lands that spread out to the horizon. She turned back to the bush, but stopped, a berry halfway to her mouth.

Beyond the bush was a dense tree line that reminded her of her dream. A forest now stood where more fields and farms had been a moment ago. Immense oak trees and smaller beech mixed with lesser trees.

Tightly packed undergrowth of strange bushes and untouched forest debris filled in between. The term 'old-growth forest' filled her head. Just like in school, a series of facts dashed through her mind like ticker-tape.

An ancient virgin forest with a diverse variety of trees.

Straight across from her was the largest oak she had ever seen. Its upper branches spread out over the canopy of the forest. The tree's trunk had to be at least twelve feet in diameter. Over a thousand years old, she calculated. Moving closer to the forest, Julia stared at the lobed leaves of the giant oak as if they were an illusion. Still not believing her own eyes, she reached out to touch one of the boughs.

A few inches from the branch, her forefinger pushed through something that felt like a puff of warm, thick gas. The air shimmered where she touched it. She yanked her hand back and studied her finger as if it had been burnt, but it was unmarked.

Julia couldn't see anything between her and the oak. Her hand trembled as she reached for the tree again. When she encountered the barrier this time, she pushed harder until her hand passed through. A ripple was created in the air, like the little waves when a stone is dropped into a pond. She could feel the heat as her hand passed through. The other side was warm, in contrast to the cool-dry winter weather on her side of the barrier.

How can this be?

She stayed for several moments, even though an incandescent light glowed around her wrist. It felt like a ring of hot metal. Determined, Julia inhaled deeply and stepped forward. The heat struck her face. It engulfed her as she went through. Julia fought to calm her rapid breathing as the searing sensation fell away and the temperature dropped to merely warm, like a spring day. Damp. The first thing she noticed when she could breathe normally was the heaviness of the air and how it hung on her body, along with the moldy smell of decaying leaves.

Silence surrounded her. The distant sound of traffic on the highway had disappeared as if a curtain had dropped between the forest and the busy route. Julia turned around and was shocked to see that the fields, her aunt's farm, and the road had vanished…replaced by thick forest. Julia panicked and forced her way through the dense undergrowth, branches slapping at her, stinging her face and hands. After several paces she stopped; her heart beat briskly.

Julia's world was gone. Everything around her felt different— not just the warmer weather, but an essence in the air and ground itself. She found her way back to the prominent oak. Turning around in a slow circle, she spotted a path. The track looked as if it had been used often. *Probably an animal trail.* It wasn't her first choice, but she didn't relish tramping through the thorny brush.

Well, I can't just sit here. Julia pushed aside branches as she worked her way down the path. Fresh droppings confirmed her guess, but the size of the piles put her on guard. She continued for over an hour, the canopy overhead thinning slightly as blotches of sunlight fell across her and the trail. The sweet, smoky, sometimes musky scents of the woods mingled with the earthy odors.

Suddenly a hoarse screech from above made her crouch.

She tried to make herself as small as possible. The shriek repeated twice, but it came from two different directions as if creatures were calling to each other. When it sounded again right overhead, she peered up through the forest's umbrella. A huge bird flew past. Its sharp talons grazed the tree tops. It was one of the hawks from her dreams. *But that's impossible!*

Julia moved quickly, but quietly, along the path. Less than half-an-hour later she came out into a clearing that was covered in waist-high grass and brush. Thin stalks shaded from green to light yellow wavered in a light breeze—a sweet smell seemed to fill the meadow. A glance around the open space didn't expose another trail. She turned to the right, resigned to finding some way through the woods, when she heard a groan to her left.

"Who's there?" she asked softly trying to keep her voice from trembling.

Another groan.

She hesitated, familiar with how dangerous a wounded animal could be.

Another long low moan came from whatever was hidden in the high grass.

It definitely sounded human.

Damn. She turned back and moved toward the distressed sound, keeping low—she felt like she was wading through water.

When Julia reached the area she thought the sound had come from, there was only silence—nothing to give her a clue where to look. She pushed the tall grass back to either side trying to find the source of the sound. As she pressed down the long shoots, she nearly stumbled over the body.

It was the silver-armored dragon rider. His blond hair draped over half his face. Fresh blood soaked the left side of his head. *Handsome, came to mind.* She quickly became alarmed as she realized another part of her dream lay before her. *How can he be here?* She moved closer and realized he looked to be only two or three years older than her, maybe twenty-one.

He moaned again when she moved his head to locate the source of the blood. A cut ran from his temple back toward his ear. It was the type of injury that could have been caused by an oversized talon, like that of the giant hawks. Julia took the arm of her coat and dabbed the wound to determine how serious it was. *Not deep.* She exhaled with relief and realized she had been holding her breath.

The screech of the hawks broke the momentary lull. *They're getting closer.*

"Crap." She looked around not sure what to do. The grass had been flattened by her steps when she'd tried to find the man. The hawk riders would easily be able to spot the two of them if they flew overhead. There wasn't anything she could do about the bent grass, but she could at least try to hide.

She couldn't imagine how she would be able to drag the wounded man into the woods, but she had to at least try. Julia dropped to one knee, grabbed him under the arms and lifted—surprised by the feel of the armor and how light it was. It looked solid, but was actually thin layers of scales, like that of…*a dragon.* The trees were only a couple of feet away, but despite the featherweight armor, it was difficult to get him over the thick trunks and through the brush. After a struggle, she managed to move him more than a dozen feet from the meadow.

The chores around the farm sure paid off. A sense of satisfaction filled her as she sat for a moment to catch her breath. She stared down at the man then back up at the clearing as her thoughts became more serious. Maybe the hawks are the good guys? Her dreams had shown her a happy people—the dragon people—no signs of aggression. She could be totally mistaken—after all, she had only seen bits and pieces in the dreams. Looking back down at him she acknowledged, "This doesn't seem like a dream." She also realized she'd already made a choice.

They'll still see the grass where I dragged him. Julia hurried back to the meadow. Julia picked up a bow left where the man had been and slung it over her shoulder. She quickly continued along the tree line making sure to push down the grass as she went. When Julia had gone twenty feet, she moved into the woods, trying to disturb the grass as little as possible. She worked her way back to the silver-armored man.

Julia crouched. She could see the clearing through a slit between two trees. The man groaned again. Julia said in a whisper to the universe, "Please. Please. Let them fly by."

A quiver of arrows was looped over the injured man's back. Julia put the bow on the ground. As gently as possible, she lifted him a little and freed his shoulder from the quiver strap. She removed her coat, took out three arrows, stuck them into the ground, then swung the rest over her own shoulder.

Another Hawk screech sounded directly overhead.

Lowering to one knee, Julia picked up the bow, thankful it wasn't a long bow. Being just over five feet tall, she would never have been able to handle one from a kneeling position.

She placed the bow in her right hand, the non-dominant one, as information began to flow into her mind. *Don't squeeze the bow too tightly—like shaking a hand.* She nocked an arrow, but didn't pull it back, leaving her left hand free.

More data continued to come to her: How to draw the bowstring back using her shoulder blades rather than just her arms; how to find an anchor point; how to shoot clearly. Somehow she knew to make sure that when she released an arrow, she would need to let her hand continue back toward the bottom of her ear to ensure all the energy in the bow would be transferred cleanly to the arrow. *Ready.* She balled her free hand into a fist to keep it from shaking.

A whoosh, then a thump, echoed over the clearing as a hawk landed.

"Celestral," the wounded man cried out in a weak voice, then fell silent again.

Julia placed her left hand lightly on his mouth and hoped he was able to understand her meaning. *Soft.* Her finger rested on his lips while her thumb grazed the light stubble on his chin. When he didn't make further sounds, she drew back the bowstring and aimed through the small opening between the trees to the clearing.

A hawk walked-hopped across the clearing and stopped in front of the slight opening between the trees. A man in blood-red armor dropped to the ground with a thud and a clang. He was tall—seven feet, maybe more, and broad in the shoulders. He wore a helmet of dark rich red marked with brown streaks. The crests on the sides of the helmet were brown as well and resembled wings in flight—hawk wings. In one hand he held an axe blade on a ten-foot-long shaft with a spike mounted on top. Halberd. Her mind identified the medieval style weapon.

The hawk rider scanned the meadow. Julia froze when he turned toward the opening, but his eyes didn't linger on the spot where she had dragged in the silver-armored rider. Instead he focused on the trampled grass path she had made and then disappeared from view.

She relaxed the bowstring and looked down at the wounded man. His head moved restlessly from side-to-side and she worried he might call out again.

A loud growl brought her head up. The hawk rider had returned. Now he peered into the shadow of the woods, sniffed again and raised the halberd, holding it diagonally across his body with both hands.

Julia pulled the bowstring back until her index finger touched the corner of her mouth—her anchor point. She took long deep breaths trying, with minimal success to calm her rapidly beating heart. *What if there are more of them?* There was little she could do now. The tip of the arrow rose slightly as she aimed just above the red-armored rider's body armor, where leather covered the man's neck.

The hawk rider lifted his head and inhaled deeply as if testing the air, then startled Julia as he let out a deep throaty snarl.

She nearly let the arrow fly at the sound, but held her breath and tried to control her shaking.

The hawk-rider pushed aside a branch and took a step into the woods.

Julia prepared to release the arrow. *Don't make me do it,* she whispered several times as she fought the fear that welled up in her.

A loud low-pitched roar shook the branches of the nearby trees and seemed to fill the sky.

The red-armored man's head snapped back to the clearing. He stepped out of the woods, turned toward his hawk. He barked several times at the giant bird, the sound shifted in pitch like a conversation, then he climbed into a saddle when the hawk lowered itself for him to mount. When he was settled in the seat, the hawk squawked and hopped out of sight.

Julia loosened the bowstring as the bird took flight. She dropped to both knees, sat back, and finally exhaled.

"The arrow wouldn't have punctured the Maynes' armor."

"That's why I aimed for the exposed neck," she answered automatically, then realized the words were from the man on the ground next to her. Julia looked down at a wide smile and a pair of sea-green eyes. *Maynes must be the hawk riders,* she decided.

He tried to push himself up with his hands, but only got as far as resting on his elbows before he cringed, his face tight. "If I could get a little help."

She walked around him, removed the bow, and got down on one knee, putting her hands under his armpits like she had in the meadow.

The armored man started to push up with his hands while she lifted. It took effort on both their parts. Finally he stood, but started to teeter until Julia grabbed his arm and barely managed to hold him up.

"I seem to be a bit shaky," he smiled again.

Julia helped him stumble over to rest against the trunk of a tree. She stood, unsure what to do as he hung his head and took a few moments to regain his breath. Everything in her dream was coming to life…and this time she was in it!

The man's head rose, sweat drenched his face. "I'm called Cordyr of the Kelrac Clan."

"I'm Julia," she answered while she picked the bow up, keeping her eyes on the man. He seemed harmless when he was unconscious. Not so much so sitting in front of her in his dragon-like armor.

He touched his head and frowned when he pulled his bloody hand away and wiped it on the leaves covering the ground. "Julia is a strange name."

"I was named after a movie star." She didn't know if that was true or not, but it was what her aunt had told her.

"Where is it?"

"I'm sorry?" Julia didn't understand the question.

"Which star?" Cordyr lifted his eyes to the covering of branches above, then looked back at her. "I'm familiar with most of the major ones in the night's sky, but never heard of one called Julia."

It took Julia a moment to realize what he was asking. "It's not that kind of a—" She sighed. This was all going horribly wrong.

"Never mind. It's not important."

Cordyr shrugged. "Well Julia. What is one of the Wolf People doing in the Myrst Forest?"

Julia just stared at him.

"Please understand, I'm not complaining." He managed a grin. "You did save my life."

"You're welcome," Julia stammered.

"It's just that your people are rarely seen this far south." The smile remained, but Julia could see him grimace as he shifted slightly.

"My people?"

"Yes. The Wolf People. From the northern regions of Entharia." A bewildered look crossed his face. "The light red hair. Pale skin. Freckles on your face and…" he hesitated, looked down her body, and cleared his throat.

Julia's cheeks warmed as her eyes dropped to the ground. She cleared her throat, looked up at him, and tried to focus on figuring out this dream…or nightmare, she wasn't sure what to call it now. "I don't know anything about Wolf People. I was having this dream—"

He sat straight, his eyes went wide and his mouth opened as if he wanted to say something, but couldn't find the words.

Julia knelt and stared into his face. "Are you okay? What's wrong?"

Her concern overcame the wariness she felt a moment before. She glanced over to check the side of his head, but it didn't look like it had started bleeding again.

"You're. A…A Dream…Dreamer!" his words came out slowly as if they were being pulled out one syllable at a time.

"It's not my fault," she complained as she sat back. How could he know? Julia's cheeks reddened again.

"You're a Dreamer," Cordyr repeated and shook his head several times. "You're a Dreamer."

"Yes I have dreams." She was becoming angry. "Everyone has dreams."

"No. You're a Dreamer," he laughed. "You…You." He pressed his lips together tightly as if frustrated. Cordyr finally found the right words, "You're a Dreamer. You can Scry."

Scry. To use divination to discover hidden knowledge, places, or future events. The definition swept through her mind and the meaning shocked her. This was like hearing a dreaded diagnosis.

She stood and turned her back to him. "But how? You say I can do these things, but how can I?"

"You're a Dreamer."

Julia bit her lip but did not turn around. She could feel her eyes welling and fought to keep from crying. *I must be going insane. This can't be true.*

"You truly don't know?" Cordyr stated, his tone tinted with disbelief. When she didn't answer, he continued in a sympathetic voice, "From time to time, a Dreamer is born among the Wolf People. Dreamers have the Sight and…well a lot of other abilities. At least that is what I've been told. I don't know a lot about the Wolf People." He paused, then added apprehensively, "Your people and mine don't get along very well."

The revelation that the Dragon People weren't friendly with the Wolf People surprised her. He seemed friendly when he first woke— which made no sense if they were at odds with each other. She wiped a sleeve across her nose as she spun around.

His wide grin and raised eyebrows made her smile. "They don't?" His greenish-blue eyes appeared to sparkle under the full brows.

"I mean we're not at war," he tried to soften his comment. "But Frore Heights is an obstacle to trade. There is little contact." He looked askance at her. "You really don't know any of this, do you?"

Julia frowned and shook her head. "I was picking berries on my aunt's farm and then this forest appeared…" She waved her hands at the trees around them. "And now I'm here. You're here. Giants in red armor riding even bigger hawks. This isn't possible."

Cordyr's lips twisted as he tried to accept what she was trying to explain. She grew quiet and stood there at a loss as to what else to do or say.

"Possible or not, we're both here and we need to get moving before the Maynes return." He grimaced, but managed to stand without her assistance. "Maybe Celestral will know more." He walked toward the clearing.

Julia automatically followed, her options limited. "Is Celestral your dragon?" She thought it was the name of a woman when he called it out earlier.

"Not mine. No one owns a dragon," he laughed without looking back.

He came to the edge of the clearing and turned back to Julia. "My guess is Celestral took my sword to draw the Maynes away."

"The dragon did have a sword when she flew toward the mountains." Julia had no idea why the sword was so important, but decided now wasn't the time to ask.

Cordyr drew a second sword, a much shorter one, from a scabbard at his side and stepped out into the clearing. "She'll come back to get me once she's lost the hawks. We'll be safe then."

Julia was still rattled by the last few hours and had no idea of what was going to happen next. She could either stick with Cordyr or…

Or what?

She walked quickly and caught up with him a dozen steps into the meadow. Julia gazed up as he scanned the sky, but the dragon wasn't in sight. They looked at each other and smiled.

A screech startled Julia and her eyes focused on the talons of a hawk that dropped like a stone toward her. A frantic thought raced through her mind, *They must have been lying in wait for us.*

Cordyr pushed Julia out of the way as the hawk landed with a thud between them as she fell.

Julia's back hurt where she had landed on the quiver, but she still managed to scramble away from the hawk and get to her feet.

She didn't drop the bow in the process.

The hawk was now riderless.

Probably attacking Cordyr.

The hawk peered at her, its eyes flicked and tracked her movements as she continued to slowly back away from it. Armor coated its chest and ran up over the neck. Something resembling a helmet wrapped around the hawk's head. There wasn't any armor over the wings. Besides the eyes and beak, the only other exposed area was a space between the throat and body, along the side, which allowed the neck to move.

With a little hop, the hawk turned toward her, its head jerked from side-to-side, then thrust forward and back as if it was examining her.

With the hawk facing her, Julia could see Cordyr. He stood opposite the much larger Maynes. They circled, but his short sword seemed trivial against the Maynes' halberd. The hawk rider swung the pole down and around horizontally. Cordyr managed to jump back, the axe blade barely missing him.

The hawk screeched, opened its wings, and hopped once in Julia's direction. The movement blocked her view of the battle on the other side.

It's trying to intimidate me.

She drew an arrow from the quiver and fumbled as she tried to get the dart nocked.

It's working.

The hawk hopped forward again.

Julia stepped another five feet backward and drew the bowstring tight. She lined up the arrow as details ran through her brain and guided her. Her hand shook even though sweat poured down the back of her neck as she aimed at the hawk's left eye. *Knowing is not the same as doing.*

When the hawk sprang forward, landing not fifteen feet from her she released the arrow. It missed the eye by a few inches and bounced off the armored helmet to strike in the exposed spot between the neck and body.

"Damn." She reached for another arrow as the hawk nipped at the shaft, seeming only irritated, not gravely wounded as she had hoped.

The hawk's head swung toward her and it screeched.

"It's pissed," she muttered while lining up the arrow again. Her hand was steady. She wasn't going to miss this time.

A loud roar filled the air above the clearing and a pair of imposing talons snagged the hawk. The bird screeched as it was wrenched violently off the ground.

The dragon lifted the hawk as the giant bird struggled unsuccessfully to break free. Celestral rose fifty feet or more over the forest, folded her wings and dropped, with the hawk still secured underneath it.

The hawk squawked in terror then let out a shrill scream as the dragon impaled the bird on the tops of several trees.

The hawk's rider squealed loudly.

Cordyr! Julia's head spun around to locate him and the Maynes.

The Maynes had evidently watched the attack as it stood shaking its halberd at the dragon.

Julia feared the red-armored rider had already killed Cordyr. She couldn't see him. The hawk rider turned in her direction as it had followed Celestral's attack and the death of its mount.

Julia jumped as the tip of a blade thrust out of the front of the hawk rider's neck, a stream of black blood spurting out with it. The blade disappeared, pulled back out.

The Maynes turned, even as blood ran down its chest, and lifted the halberd above its head.

It was then that Julia saw Cordyr, a shocked expression on his face, as he held the bloody sword with both hands ready to try and deflect the axe blade.

Rather than swing the long poled-blade, the Maynes stood for a moment, then dropped to both knees and finally fell forward onto its face.

Cordyr's body relaxed and he exhaled. The sword dropped to rest at his side.

Julia looped the bow over her back, and ran over to throw her arms around him. She put her head against his chest and squeezed tightly. "You're all right." At some point, she wasn't sure when, Julia had come to trust the dragon rider—and there was something else—a new, different feeling in her stomach. A tightness, but it didn't feel bad.

At first he put one arm around her. "Yes." Then he put the other one around and her heart quickened.

They stayed like that until he asked, "You seem to be safe."

"Yes," she answered with a smile, then realized what she was doing and backed away. She'd only just met this man. *I don't know anything about him. Grow up Julia!* She rationalized that having been near death might be the cause of these sudden emotions.

"I...I." Before she could come up with an excuse, the flapping of giant wings sounded and wind swept over the meadow. Her head jerked to the side as Celestral landed and filled much of the clearing.

Once on the ground, the dragon took several steps toward them. Julia noticed it walked quietly on the front of its paws like a cat. She had glimpsed the dragon in her dreams, but this was the first time she had seen it this close. Short horns rose like antlers from its head and a raised spine ridge ran down the back of its neck. The wings were bat-like, attached near the bottom of the back, close to the thighs.

Julia's mind quickly did an anatomical and air dynamic analysis, concluding that it was optimal construct to allow the dragon to fly horizontally. It would provide for greater maneuverability with the head and tail as a rudder, and a greater surface for the wings to capture the wind. The data that flowed through her head also calculated that it should be impossible for the dragon to fly, considering its size. She smiled. *This dragon should be impossible to begin with.*

Its head swung in her direction—its eyes narrowed as if scrutinizing her before it shifted to Cordyr.

Julia stepped closer to the man.

A claw appeared from under the wing and held out Cordyr's longsword, the same one that had looked as if afire in her dream.

"Dragon's Fire." A wide grin spread across Cordyr's face as he took the sword. He inspected it as he turned it from side-to-side before he slid it into the scabbard on his back.

A low-pitched voice entered her head, "Did the female hurt you?"

Somehow she knew the voice violating her mind was that of the dragon talking to Cordyr.

"I didn't hurt him." She was offended by the dragon's accusation.

The dragon turned quickly, ending with its snout only a few feet from her. Julia jumped.

'The female heard me.'

"Yes. I guess I did." Julia didn't feel as bold with the dragon's fangs so close.

Celestral's head jutted closer; the dragon sniffed, then pulled back. "I don't like the smell of this female," the dragon spoke clearly, in a voice that wasn't much different from what Julia had heard in her mind.

I don't stink. Her anger was building again. She'd never met a dragon before, but was beginning to take a definite dislike to this one.

"She may have been sent by the Red Witch, Asmerilda." Celestral's mouth opened wider so her long fangs were prominent.

Julia felt her heart jump when the dragon added, "Should I kill her?"

"No! No! No!" Cordyr stepped in front of Julia, both hands held up to stop the dragon. "She saved my life."

Celestral stared at her rider before returning her attention to Julia.

"Are you from the Red Witch?"

"Who's the Red Witch?" Julia stayed glued to Cordyr. His armor was cool to the touch, she was comforted just being near him. She wasn't surprised that her mind remained empty of information. Her unique ability didn't seem to apply to people.

"She lies!" The dragon's head shot to within a foot of Cordyr. Julia stepped back, but he didn't flinch.

"After eighteen years, Asmerilda has returned." Celestral's neck swung around to the side so she could glare at Julia. "Everyone knows of the Red Witch."

"She doesn't." Cordyr moved to put himself between Julia and the dragon again. "She doesn't know." He paused, glanced over his shoulder at Julia with a smile, then back at Celestral, and added, "She's a Dreamer."

The dragon's neck whipped up and back so that its head towered over them. It stared down examining Julia, its horizontal eyelids partially closed, shrinking the vertical slits of the dragon's pupils to a size a little larger than Julia's fist.

'A Dreamer?' The dragon's thoughts entered Julia's mind before it spoke to her, "Are you of the Wolves?"

"She's never heard of them either," Cordyr answered for her.

I can speak for myself, Julia wanted to say, but still appreciated him defending her.

"Yes. Let her speak for herself," Celestral told Cordyr.

The dragon can hear my thoughts!

"Yes," the irritation in Celestral's tone made the dragon seem more threatening.

Julia didn't want to anger the large dragon, but the idea that someone could read her thoughts seemed scarier than the hawks.

"Where did you come from?" Celestral lowered her head, the dragon's maw close enough that Julia could feel heat and an odor that reminded her of burning wood or charcoal.

"Back in the forest." Julia pointed behind her without looking. "I was picking berries on my aunt's farm when the forest appeared. It wasn't there..." Julia knew she must sound crazy and the dragon would think she was lying. "Then it was. It just appeared from…nowhere."

Celestral's head rose again and nodded from more than fifteen feet above Julia, then confirmed what she had been told, "You are a Dreamer. Only a Dreamer can cross Between."

"Between?" Cordyr asked.

"Between worlds," Julia was startled by her own voice as the information ran through her mind. *One of the abilities of a Dreamer is to traverse the boundaries between worlds.* It frustrated Julia that only this one item would pop into her head, when what she needed was other information about what a Dreamer was or facts that might help her out right now.

"I don't understand." Cordyr's focus bounced from Julia to Celestral, then back again.

Celestral lowered to the ground, her tail wrapped around her body. Settled, the dragon explained, "The Dreamer, Julia, came from one of the other worlds."

"Other worlds?" Cordyr shook his head slowly.

Julia could sympathize with him, as that was how she had been feeling for the last few hours, enveloped in a peculiar mix of shock and confusion. Wait a minute. She scowled at Celestral. *I never told her my name.*

The dragon only tilted its head and returned the look.

Oh, that makes sense. She imagined the dragon had plucked it from Cordyr's mind.

"This is but one of several worlds." Celestral didn't elaborate.

Cordyr began to say something, but his voice faded and he seemed far away, as if he was at the other end of a tunnel. A spider web had fallen over Julia's eyes, at least it felt that way as her vision became fuzzy, then disappeared altogether.

She was looking down at the top of the trees, but could tell it was a different part of the forest. Ten hawks winged into view with their red-armored riders. At the front of their formation was an enormous beast that had the body of a hawk but the head of a bear. Another armored rider rode the bear-hawk. The rider was smaller than the others with similar red armor, but the glint of gold trim flashed in the partial sun. Long red robes flowed behind the rider; its helmet was twice as tall as the other riders'. Gold wing crests sprouted from either side and it looked as if flames poured off them.

The image disappeared as quickly as it had arrived.

"Julia. Julia. What is it?" Cordyr held her by the arms and looked intently into her eyes as they opened.

"The Red Witch," she stammered softly, then blurted in a frenzy, "It's the Red Witch. She's coming."

"We delayed too long," Celestral chastised. Her tail whipped around behind her. "Mount."

Cordyr held out a hand to Julia, his easy smile drawing her in. "Come with us to the castle. You'll be safe there."

A familiar scene of the castle rose from the back of her mind—a celebration of some type and she smiled.

Cordyr's grin widened, but her smile faded as her feet refused to move. She pictured her elderly aunt. The woman never stopped complaining and seemed intent on making Julia's life miserable. Yet, no one had made her aunt raise her—that must mean something. *What would my disappearance do to her heart?*

"Hurry." Cordyr waved her toward him—his tone uneasy and the smile gone, replaced with a worried expression.

"I can't." She couldn't believe she was saying the words. "I can't go with you. This isn't my world." Tears ran down her cheeks and her body shook.

"Come with me." His greenish-blue eyes pleaded.

"We must go. The Red Witch approaches." Celestral put out a front leg and urged Cordyr to step up and on to her back.

"We have to go, Julia." He took a step toward her, but she held up a hand to stop him.

Through sobs she managed to tell him, "I can't. I have to go home." She still had a few months before graduating and her aunt was counting on her around the farm—at least until she finished high school. Julia's grades would get her into a state college, tuition-free.

Cordyr stared intently at her, his jaw tight. The sorrow in his eyes broke her heart. He ran up the dragon's leg and jumped into the oversized saddle. "We will lead them away. Go back along the path." A light smile crossed his lips and he added, "I will be looking for your return. In the meantime keep me in your dreams."

She tried to smile back and wiped the tears from her cheeks. "I will." She didn't know exactly what she meant, the words just spilled out.

Celestral rose to her paws as Julia backed up toward the trail.

The dragon's neck straightened and her head lifted to the sky. Her face turned toward Julia. "All Dreamers are born of this world. No other."

"That can't be. I've never been here…just in my dreams," she added.

Celestral flapped her wings once, then a second time, making Julia cover her eyes and step into the path's opening.

"You were born here. Dreamers' mothers are Dreamers. One came to the Dragon People and mated with Lord Tolucan. They bore a child who disappeared when the Red Witch first came." Celestral crouched cat-like, the tendons in her legs knotted as she prepared to spring into the air.

"What happened to them?" *My parents! Could it be?* Her emotions raged as confusion clouded her thoughts.

"They went to battle the Red Witch." The dragon looked up again. "They never returned nor did the Red Witch…until now." Celestral leapt above the tree tops, wings beating as she rose higher.

Julia was buffeted by the whirlwind, and nearly knocked down.

"Come back. My parents—," she yelled, but the dragon and rider were already heading away from the clearing. "My parents," she said softly.

The sound of many wings came from the opposite direction.

Julia edged back onto the trail where she believed she wouldn't be noticed and watched the hawks she had seen in her latest vision.

In the front was the Red Witch on her bear-hawk. She appeared to be turning to follow the dragon.

A sharp pain struck Julia, as if an explosion had gone off in the center of her mind. She dropped to her knees and put both hands to her head.

'Block her,' a strange female voice encouraged in her thoughts. *'She is looking for you.'*

How, Julia screamed, the word bounced throughout her head.

Julia glanced up and squinted—her head felt as if someone were driving a red hot iron through it.

The Red Witch had turned to circle around the meadow, looking down into woods.

Julia scrambled on her hands and knees further back along the path.

Hide your mind. Focus on what you want, the voice urged.

The image of Cordyr, and his wide smile filled her with a comfort she had never felt in the past. His hand was held out, as it was when he asked her to come with them.

A globe of bright light appeared in her mind. It enclosed the red iron and began to grow smaller. The pain subsided as the sphere continued to contract. When the ball had shrunk to a dot, the iron and the pain disappeared.

An anguished scream came from above the clearing, and Julia heard the sound of the hawks passing overhead again as they quickly winged away.

"Who are you?" Julia questioned the mysterious voice, but no response came. She waited a few minutes to make sure the Red Witch wouldn't return and also to catch her breath after the pain had nearly paralyzed her.

When Julia's breathing returned to normal, she rushed up the path until she came to the smaller clearing where the huge oak tree stood. She hesitantly approached the tree and put her hand on the trunk. The forest to her left, beyond the oak, became translucent, then disappeared altogether, revealing the fields and her aunt's farm.

Julia stepped toward the familiar landscape and in a few steps encountered the barrier. She stood there for several moments, a battle raging within her. In the distance, like through the wavy haze of a hot summer day, she could see her aunt driving up to the farm in a car that was only slightly younger than the elderly woman.

Julia's hand shot forward as if she could reach her aunt; it breached the barrier. An intense cold encircled her wrist like a band of ice. She didn't stop but stepped through, trying not to let any of her thoughts deter her. The air on the other side was like she remembered from earlier in the day. It was cold and felt barren in contrast to the warmth and feeling of being alive she felt in the other world.

Other world. The thought still seemed foreign to her.

She spun around and as she had feared, the forest was gone. Nothing but more fields and a few farms on the horizon filled her view.

"Julia," her aunt yelled at the house as she exited the car. "Come help me with these groceries."

Her aunt still had not noticed Julia in the field. With a sigh and a shrug, Julia took a step toward the ranch house. The bowstring pulled taut across her chest and she realized that the bow was still slung over her shoulder along with the quiver.

With the bow and quiver in her hands Julia, scanned around for someplace to hide them. *The barn.* Bales of hay were stacked behind it. She ran before her aunt saw her. Out of breath Julia found a crevice between the bales and the rear wall. She grabbed a small tarp from a pile next to the bale, covered the weapons, and shoved them as far as she could into the opening. The sweet smell of the hay filled her nostrils even as broken stalks made little cuts in her hand.

Still breathing heavily, she raced around the house to the front.

"Taking your time girl," her aunt's sarcastic tone didn't bother her...anymore. "And where's your coat? You'd think you were smart enough to know it's still cold outside."

"I'll look for it after I help you with the groceries." *But I won't find it.* She hurried over to get the bags out of the trunk.

"Where were you?" Her aunt's forehead wrinkled and her eyes narrowed—an expression Julia was extremely familiar with.

"I looked around for you earlier. You were to go to the store, but you had disappeared," her aunt continued as Julia carried the bags up to the porch.

Julia froze at the doorway, the screen open, and flinched when her aunt moved past her and pushed the door open.

"Never mind. Probably off day dreaming again." Her aunt stepped through and held the door open, her finger waggled at Julia who followed. "If you don't get your act together girl, you'll never make it out there. This is a cold, hard world we live in."

The next morning, Julia awoke with the sun, disappointed and exhausted. It had been a dreamless night and she had not slept well. She had gone to bed early hoping to find out if Cordyr and Celestral had made it safely back to the castle.

She lay there for a while, the worry ever present as she tried to fall back asleep, to dream. Her aunt's call to morning chores dispelled any hope that might happen.

She didn't move for a few more moments as questions filled her thoughts. *Was it all part of the dream?* Cordyr and the dragon felt so real. She could still see the color of his eyes, the grin that was both funny and sweet. But another world! It seemed impossible. Celestral's thoughts in her mind along with that of the strange female voice. It all seemed so real. *But it can't be.*

Julia washed up and dressed as the arguments continued to make her wonder if she was truly going insane. Heading down the stairs, rationalization had taken over. *My life's so miserable I have to escape into these crazy dreams.* She was a fool to think otherwise, though thinking of Cordyr and the other world made her feel warm in the chill of the early morning. *I'll take what I can get.*

"Collect the eggs," her aunt ordered without looking up.

Julia went to the back door, but her coat wasn't on the peg. My coat! She had forgotten. The door banged shut behind her. Her face and neck stung in the cold, her long sleeves doing little to keep her chest and arms warm.

Hoping, but not believing, she ran around the side of the barn to the rear where the hay bales were stacked. Julia approached slowly the small crevice near the ground between one of the bales and the back wall.

What if they're not there? Her heart beat faster and faster. Julia knelt and took a minute to calm down, inhaling and exhaling deeply. Her hand shook as she reached into the crevice.

A tarp. Her hand rubbed across the rough material. Julia yanked it toward her and could feel something wrapped in it. The tarp came out and she laid it next to the bale, then slowly unrolled it to expose the bow and quiver of arrows.

"I knew it," she shouted, happier than she could ever remember.

"What are you doing out there Julia?" her aunt called impatiently from the back door on the other side of the barn.

"Checking on the chickens," she yelled back. The barn hid her aunt's view of the coop.

"Just get the eggs and get yourself in here."

Julia quickly rewrapped the bow and quiver, then shoved it back into the crevice. Later she would find a better hiding place, one close to somewhere she could practice in private. *Knowing is not the same as doing,* she reminded herself. She still had a few months until graduation. Enough time to feel confident with the weapon. A smile filled her face as she thought, *I'll need to be proficient with these if I'm going to return.*

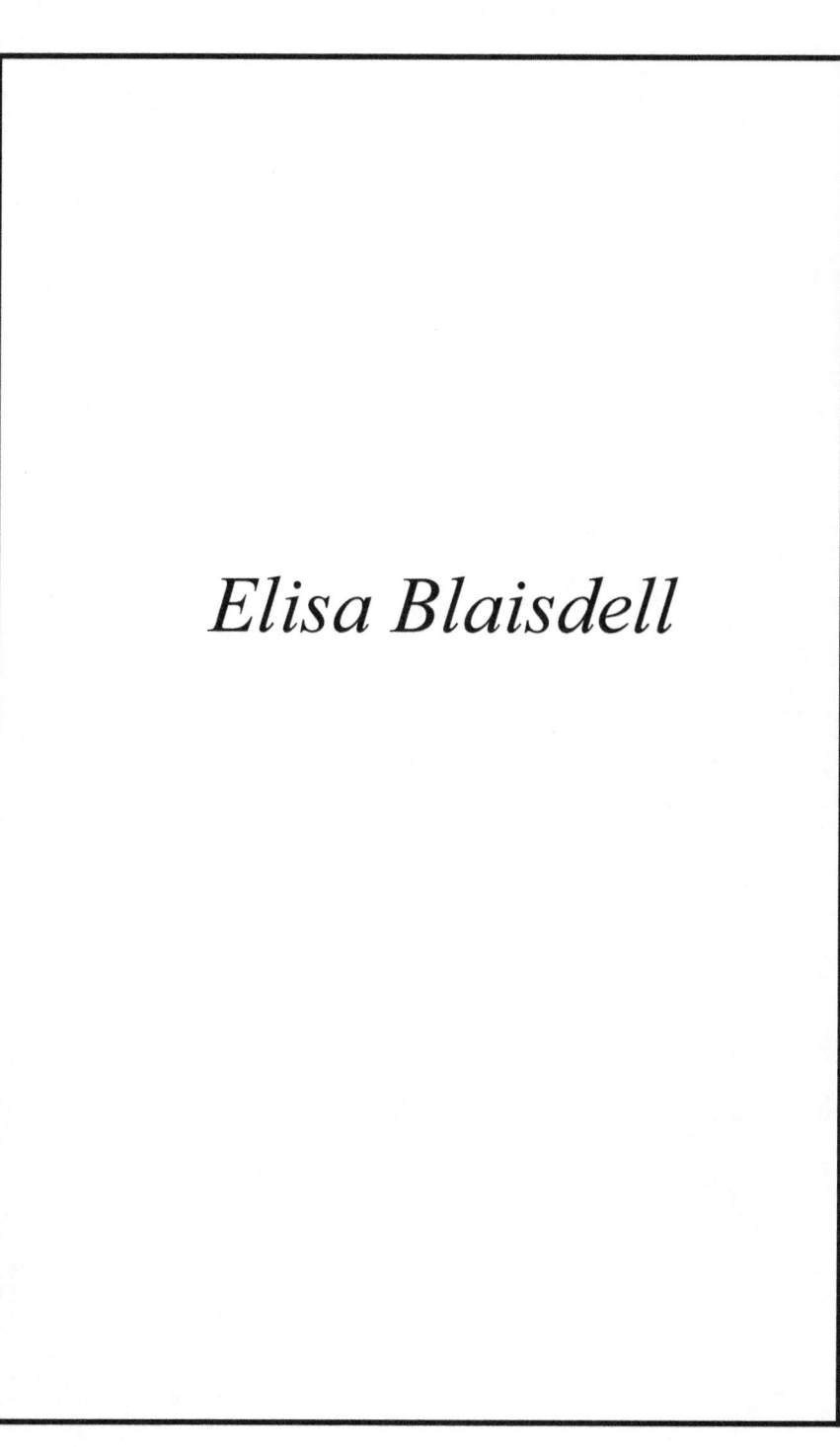

Elisa Blaisdell

TO THE ROCKS

I think that my lord first made his plan on the night that we attended his nephew's showing. The great hall shone with torchlight. All of the city nobles had come. I had dressed for the occasion as though it were one of rejoicing, putting on a gown of deep blue lanara silk, embroidered with tiny sweetsnow flowers, and setting blue stones at my throat and my ears. I think that none of the women there outdazzled me, however younger they might be.

The father stripped off his son's wrappings. The baby squirmed and wailed lustily in the chill air. "Fine lungs," my lord whispered to me.

"This is the measure of a man," the baby's father recited. "Observe his eyes, his nose, his ears." We dutifully observed. "Observe his hands, with five fingers on each." The baby clenched those five fingers into fists, and howled louder as his father tried to stretch them out to display to us. I bit my lower lip until the blood ran, then quickly blotted it with my kerchief before anyone could notice. My lord's eyes were fixed upon the baby. I tried to read his expression, and could not.

"His skin is without blemish." The boy's mother watched the ceremony, her face so filled with joy that you might have thought it ready to burst into flames.

"His limbs are straight and as they should be." An arc of urine sprayed through the air, staining the father's white robes. "Observe that all his parts work as they should," my lord whispered to me. I smiled dutifully..

"I have read the measure of a man," the father concluded. "Is this a man?"

"This is a man," we replied in unison.

***

Afterwards there was feasting and laughter. I ate my fill—I think that food may be my greatest pleasure, nowadays. The doves simmered in sweet spices were especially good, as was the thornfruit candy, hot from the oven. Then, we stepped into separate litters, my lord and I, and were lifted up for the journey home. Our bearers carried us side by side so we could talk, but my lord said not one word, nor did I. I sensed his gray eyes look toward me. Several times, I heard the sigh of his breath, as though he wished to begin to speak, but he was silent.

I spoke at last of mundane things, when we reached our home with its dim torches burning in the courtyard. "I am weary. I will go to my room now."

"Rest well, my dear," he said, as he lifted my hand to kiss it. I went to my room, tired in truth. My servants dressed me in bed-silks, and left. I waited, but he did not come to my room, and I was glad. At last, I slept.

***

My lord traveled out to the forest the next day, riding with his troop of soldiers, a fine display. He patrols there every year before summer comes. From what he has said, it serves no real purpose except to let all know that the king's power extends to every corner and winding trail of his land.

I passed the time in the usual way, while he was gone. I sat with my hands, with their long curling fingernails, clasped in my lap, as I watched my maidservants work and listened to them gossip and prattle.

"They say that the forest is filled with monsters," Lilla said with a delighted shiver as she set neat stitches in a length of silk. "Ones that can change their shape to beautiful women, to lure men to their deaths."

"Hah!" said Sidene, older and confident. "How many years has our lord ridden to the forest and returned safely home?"

I remembered when I first came to this palace, in a marriage arranged by many messenger doves flying weary flights from distant lands. We traveled through the forest, a strange place with its dim green light, but I saw no danger in it. I was young.

In those early days, Sidene herself looked at me askance, and made signs to ward off evil spirits. I wore the black hair of an accursed southerner then. Now that my hair is as white as hers, she seems to have forgotten her fears.

So a sevendays passed, and then one afternoon there was a shouting in the courtyard. "Our lord has returned!"

My heart leaped with joy, and I sprang up from my chair. Then I composed myself, and walked sedately out to greet him. He sat astride his brown gelding, his face unshaven and weary. But behind him, a woman—a girl—sat pillion. Young, with long black hair and the sly dark eyes of a witch. He dismounted, lifted her down, and came to me.

"Greetings, my lady, my wife," he said, as he lifted my hand to his lips. "This is Lenane, whom I have brought from the forest, and who is now my wife."

I think I was gracious. I do not remember what I said. That was a lesson my mother never taught me—how to greet the woman who has supplanted you. But habit is a kindly thing, to carry us along, and offering a weary guest a bath, clean clothes, and food are simple enough things to do.

At the table, I did not ask questions. His first words had told me all I wanted to know. She ate daintily, but ate much. Roast grasskit stuffed with grain and savory vegetables. Cakes sweetened with thornfruit honey, and sharpened with just a trace of bittery to keep the honey from cloying. In time, she will be as stout as I am, I thought. Her eyes looked everywhere, appraising everything. That little smile was always on her lips. She said nothing.

My lord seemed to try to look at neither of us, but after we had finished, he spoke to her.

"Sing for us, Lenane."

Her smile became larger. "What would you hear?"

"Whatever you choose."

Her speech was sweet-toned enough. Still, I hoped for a croaking song. She took a breath, and began.

Her song told the story that all know, how the great gray dragon, Yvaressinest, was enchanted, tamed, and chained, brought to Mareja, kingdom of the sea, to satisfy the whim of a princess.

Her voice began sweet, but then it swelled, as she sang of the patient anger of the dragon. My spine shivered and the hair on my arms stood on end. Her voice became harsh but still beautiful, as she told of his great teeth gnawing his leg free of its fetter. It soared in frightening joy as his long wings lifted him into the air, and then as he swooped and dived on the frightened townspeople, breathing his deadly fire, taking his revenge. It died in an eerie whisper as he soared out over the ocean, flying west to the land from which he had been stolen, flying west, maimed but free.

I could not praise her immediately, although I wished to. My breath was still caught in my throat, and my thoughts were spinning wildly. My lord spoke first with a voice full of pride, pride of ownership, I thought, and then I no longer wished to praise her. "Very nice," I said finally, in a flat little voice that did not even sound like my own.

She sang other ballads, ones I did not know. Each one beguiled me, against my will. Is this how she bewitched my lord? I asked myself. Then I looked at her black hair falling far past her shoulders, and at her body, as supple as a lacewood tree, as mine was once, before ten dead children. No, she had no need of her voice to bewitch him.

I thanked her at last, and left the hall, so I did not have to wait and see her go to her room, and watch him follow her. In my room, once my maidservants had left me, I crushed my face into the pillow, as though I were trying to smother myself, as though I were trying to keep myself from hearing the sound of my own weeping.

The next day I asked her to join me on a trip to the market street. You would have thought that a litter was some strange torture device, if you judged from the way she shied and balked. I used the stern voice that I would have used on a servant, to tell her that our lord's honor required that we travel in dignity.

"Travel?" she said in a startled voice, but she obeyed, stepped onto the platform, seated herself in the chair, even arranged her hands in her lap in a manner that resembled mine so closely that it could have been mockery.

Near the entrance to the street, a catlen girl danced. I told the bearers to stop and let us watch. The dancer's fair hair was cut short and curled on her neck; her skirt and overblouse were ragged. She stepped forward gracefully, and with every step she flexed her raised hands, making metal claws flash as they sprang out from the bracelets welded around her fragile wrists. Then the claws slid back into their slots on her wrist, another step, and they flashed out in a sharp-hooked warning, again and again as she danced forward.

Lenane laughed with a little catch of breath. "It would be wise to not anger her!"

"Did you see such sights in the forest?" I asked.

"I had not lived there always," she said, and then looked startled at having said something about herself. "And yes, I have seen such sights, but it pleases me to see them again."

Before we left, I had the bearers drop a handful of red-metal coins into the catlen's basket.

When we reached the street, we alighted, so that we could enter the shops. Lenane said nothing as we looked at lengths of embroidered silk, but I could see by her eyes that this was not something she had seen before, in whatever place she came from. Although my storerooms have a wealth of cloth, on an impulse I pointed toward one, deep pink, embroidered with stars.

"This one, for you. You will need fine clothes, now." Her smile gleamed sincerely.

Later, the storekeeper said as he wrapped it, "An excellent choice! It suits your daughter's coloring well." Her smile glinted mockingly then.

We walked on down the street, the bearers following us closely, waiting for the time when we grew weary with walking or simply weary with looking.

An herbalist stood in his doorway, calling his stocks. "Herbs to heal, herbs to harm! Herbs to help bear children, and herbs to guard against their being born! All manner of herbs for every heart's desire!"

We walked on down the street, and with his chant of "Herbs to heal, herbs to harm!" still ringing in my ears, I glanced at her, and saw that she was watching me, her dark eyes unreadable.

I thought of the other time I visited the herbalist's shop. Sure enough as he promised, I bore a child who lived and breathed—for a while. Never again! I will not buy his wares, ever again!

***

Time passed, in almost ordinary ways. As I listened to Lenane singing in the evening, I tried to not think of my lord going to her room when the singing ended. I had wished to be free of his attentions, but I had not known how lonely the nights would be. I used lotions to keep my eyes bright and clear, with no sign of my tears.

In time, my lord rode out to the forest again. I tried to treat Lenane as though I cared for her, hoping that fantasy might turn to truth. As I showed her the cloth chests, and said she might choose what she wished, I tried to pretend that she was indeed my daughter, grown tall and beautiful. Then a sideways glance from her eyes, a mocking tone in her overly-respectful voice, destroyed the illusion.

One morning, a commotion in the courtyard brought me out. Lenane rushed ahead of me, and then stopped and retreated when she saw a stranger. Jerrid was no stranger to me, my lord's youngest brother, born of his father's second wife a year after my lord and I were married. He had grown to be a fine man, though not quite as handsome as my lord.

I saw a sparkle of interest in his eyes as I introduced him to Lenane. At the evening meal I said little, only asking him a few questions, that he might speak, and shine, and catch her interest. Afterward, I asked her to sing, hoping that her voice would beguile him.

That worked better than I had hoped. I had not realized that he loved music so. He seized a lute from the wall, and strummed to join her singing. Then, he asked her if she played also, and when she shook her head, he took the lute to her, pressed it into her hands, and set himself to showing her how her fingers should lie on the strings.

I thought of excusing myself then, and leaving them to themselves. Let palms pat against palms, and eyes gaze into eyes, and breaths mingle. Who knew what might happen, and when my lord returned home, he might find something that would anger him, and make him cast her aside.

I dreamed of it. I wanted it to happen, but I could not bring myself to leave. As I watched them, I saw how Lenane's eyes avoided his, how her body shifted slightly away from him as he leaned toward her. Witch she might be, but no wanton. And besides, the music was beautiful. Why should I deprive myself of it?

So, evening after evening, I kept guard over them, and listened to their music. On the day that Jerrid left, he kissed my hand, and I saw wry amusement in his eyes, as though he understood my thoughts.

***

I knew it, before she realized it. The signs were easy enough. One morning she left the table without eating, and the next, I found her retching desperately into a bucket.

I took her long black hair gently, and pulled it back to safety. "Be glad, little one. You are with child."

When she could speak, she turned to me, her eyes gleaming with mischief. "And here I feared you had poisoned me at last!"

I turned and left her then, so I would not be tempted to slap her insolent face.

As she grew heavier, the sickness left her. Our days took a new pattern. I sat as before, hands folded in my lap, watching my maidservants. Lenane played the lute endlessly, sometimes picking out tunes, often just playing endless notes in sequences of fast and slow, loud and soft. Once I said, "You should grow your fingernails long, like mine, to show your rank."

"It would mar my fingers for the lute strings," she said. I did not insist. I looked forward to the evenings, more and more, as her lute playing began to join with her voice to create new wonders of ancient lands and forbidden magic.

At last her time came. She whimpered sometimes, screamed

sometimes. My lord, back safely from the forest, kept a discreet distance, fearing lest all we women should turn on him and blame him for her pain.

"A boy!" my maidservant Sidene said with delight. The baby did not need to be coaxed or slapped into life. He wailed vigorously as she held him up. Then she gasped, and our eyes met.

"Take him away, and do what is necessary," I whispered. "Show him to our lord, so he knows."

She nodded and left. Lenane's eyes were closed. I hoped she would sleep. But she stirred to life and reached out her hand.

"Where is my child?"

"Later, later. Sleep now."

"Where is he?" Her voice filled with frightened urgency, and she tried to sit up.

I pressed her shoulders back against the pillows, and looked up at my other maidservant. "Lilla, run and get help!" She turned and obeyed, eager to leave the room.

Lenane fought me until I feared she would harm herself. Then my lord rushed in and held her down. He had the courage—or foolishness—to tell her. "His foot was twisted, so that the heel would never touch the ground. He would never meet the measure of a man." Then he continued in sheer foolishness. "Have courage. You will bear more, and they will be fine and strong."

As I did? I thought in fury. She screamed wordlessly. She tried to claw his face. Our menservants held her down, as my lord fled the room. Then they tied her hands and feet to the bed, so she could not harm herself. I stayed, and tried to calm her. Her screaming continued, and grew hoarser. She twisted her body, trying to fight loose from her bonds. I feared that she might bleed more than she should. I touched her hair, her shoulder, trying to comfort her.

I said nothing. What could I say? That I had five children who died in my womb, and four who failed and faded after they were born ... and first of all, one who was strong and healthy, a little black-haired girl, screaming in fury at the world from the moment she entered it. Her fingers were longer than they should have been, and webbing stretched between them, like the feet of some water bird. She did not meet the measure of a man—I knew that when I first saw her—and she was sent to the rocks.

Lenane still tried to scream, mouth open, and gasping for more air, but no sound came from her lips. I left the room at last, telling myself in cowardice that she might rest better alone.

The second day, she did not fight or scream, and she ate a little— grasskit broth with puffed blaggorn kernels soaked in it. She said nothing. The third day, we dared to untie her.

She lay passively, looking from side to side, her eyes unfocused. Thinking that she might rest better alone, I left her. After an hour, I looked in on her. She was gone.

We all rushed out, I, my lord, our servants, hurrying in different directions. I forgot the dignity of being carried in a litter. I am glad I was not the one who found her—I do not know what I would have done. One of our manservants, searching wisely, found her collapsed and half hidden at the side of the path that leads to the rocks. He carried her back, her night-silks stained with the blood that her womb wept. We tied her again, and waited, day after day. That she continued to eat was enough victory for us.

She first spoke to me as I fed her broth, her voice hoarse and almost soundless. "Untie me. I know that he is dead."

I did not dare do it, but I called for my lord to come and speak with her. I do not know what she said, but she convinced him that she was sane again, and we released her.

She grew stronger and rose from her bed. She paced through the hallways and courtyard as though she were trying to wear herself to exhaustion. Then she took the lute from the wall, not playing it now and not singing—her voice still so hoarse that she could hardly breathe a word to us. Now she played one note, over and over, louder, softer, louder again, till my nerves were ready to snap. But I said nothing.

I think my lord was glad when the king sent him to ride out through the land again. He kissed us both goodbye, but he turned quickly to mount his gelding, and he set a brisk pace to lead his men out the gate.

"How long till he returns?" Lenane whispered to me that evening at dinner.

"A ten days or more," I replied. Something flickered in her eyes. For the first time, I read her thoughts.

The next day, I had Sidene distract her while I slipped into her room. Her preparations were far along, already. She had kept the pack she carried when she arrived. It was hidden under the bed. Food, stolen from table and larder, was wrapped in coarse cloth taken from my storechests. The rags that she wore when she came were laundered clean and rolled neatly. I touched something hard, unrolled it. A gold cup taken from the hall chest. Inside the coarser wrappings, a length of white silk, embroidered with many-colored flowers. I thought for a minute, then went to my own room, and returned with a handful of coins knotted into my kerchief. I tucked it into a corner of the pack.

As she stepped through her door and caught me at my snooping, I felt as guilty as a thief, but I faced her and met her eyes. "When are you leaving?"

"Tomorrow," she whispered.

"Do you have all you need?"

"Almost."

I stepped out into the great hall. She must have expected me to shout for the servants, for her eyes widened when I returned, lute in hands. "Take this with you."

She nodded. "Will you go with me to the rocks?"

I caught my breath, but I had done the same once, myself, and it had helped me. So, the next day, the bearers carried us in litters, side by side, out to the rocks. Bones of old deaths were scattered across the plain. In the distance, golden vultures swirled, descended, and rose again. The bearers carried us closer, close enough to see that someone full grown had died of sickness or age. I looked out across the stony plains. Glints of white here and there. He had been such a little thing, and the carrion creatures are greedy. How do you tell one child's bones from another's?

"He is dead," I said.

She met my eyes. "He is dead," she whispered.

So we let the bearers carry us back to the city. There, I stood by her side. She sobbed with agony as the metalsmith welded claws onto her slim wrists.

"Now, you carry your defenses with you always," he said, as he finished. *The scars of that burning she will carry always,* I thought.

At the edge of the city, I told the bearers to let her descend, and I watched her as she walked into the distance and disappeared, her lute slung across her shoulders.

Then they brought me home.

My lord will go to the forest many more times, I know. When he brings home another wife, may she be more fortunate than we have been.

As I wait for his return, to face his anger, I think again of how I stood by her at the herbalist's and said not one word, as she whispered hoarsely: "Give me herbs to eat, that I may never bear another child."

Rice Canyon, 2007

On October 22, 2007, strong winds blew a sycamore limb down across electric
lines, starting a fire that burned 206 homes and 9400 acres of land.

Power lines pour sparks into the windy night.
A pillar of flames rises from dry grass.
There is no way out.

Chaparral hillsides, rich with oil
that saved them through this drought.
Sheets of embers overhead,
fireworks better than I have ever seen.
There is no way out.

I climb down the hill to pools of dragonfly polliwog memories.
This creek has given people life for centuries.
I wade into those precious inches of water.
My feet sink into the mud.

He shall give his angels charge over you,
to keep you in all your ways.
Wherever an ember falls, a fire kindles, rises, joins with others.
The air burns in my nose, and the smoke grows thicker.

A thousand may fall at your side,
and ten thousand at your right hand,
but it shall not come near you.
There is no life in this air,
and fires burn in the treetops now.

"Lord, if I live, I will do things differently."
My bargaining thoughts shame me.
I have lived so alone, and who will care if I die?
Some, a few, enough.

I set my head on a small pillow of sand.
I pull up my skirt to mask my face.
My cupped hands splash coldness over me,
as steadily as swimming.
I take shallow breaths of the worthless air.

This water is deathly cold. I reach out my hands
to warm them at the wall of flame,
then angrily return to slapping the stings of ember mosquitoes.

The creek mutters in my ears in languages
I've never known.
Red light shines through my closed eyelids.
One more breath, one handful of water over my face,
one more, one more.

Now the air has some life again,
and the sky is a paler gray.
Does anyone else live in this burned world?

Footsteps in ashes are silent.
I turn and meet the kind bewildered eyes of firemen,
and so they lead me out through ashes
back to life.

THE CRIME SCENE

I was just home from my first year of college, planning a summer of long hours spent playing the piano and reading worthy books. Late that morning, I turned on the faucet in the kitchen and no water came out. No cause for dismay—it was just a little lack of planning. I trudged down our long dirt driveway to turn on the pump that pulled water from the well on the other side of the road. It pumped it up to the reservoir on the hill, to provide us with a gravity-powered semblance of water pressure.

I flipped the switch. The pump came on with a satisfying growl. I strolled back toward the house, wiping summer sweat off my forehead. And there, below the ledge at the side of our driveway, lay a dead dog—a large black Labrador. Really dead? Most certainly he was, stiff, already smelling a little, and huge green flies starting to show an interest in him.

My shock and sympathy were quickly pushed out of the way by a certain self-centered practicality. *What do I do? I buried my own dog last summer, and it was a horrible job. I'm not going to do that for a strange dog!*

As far as I knew, none of my neighbors owned a black Labrador. No recourse there. Government agencies? A long shot, but worth a try. Back at the house, I dug into the Yellow Pages. Animal Control—that sounded promising. And, they were astonishingly helpful.

"We'll charge you forty dollars to pick the dog up off your property," the voice on the other end of the line said. "But, if he's out at the

216

road, there's no cost."

Forty dollars…. I thought of the number of dorms vacuumed and wastebaskets emptied it took to earn that much money, back at college. But was this really honest? I needed clarity.

"Do you mean that I can move him out to the road? That'll be okay? You'd pick him up for free? That's all right with you?"

"Yes."

"Okay, he'll be out there in two hours." *That's much more time than I need, but always good to be conservative.*

I recruited my mother. She wasn't strong enough to do the dirty work, but she knew where everything was kept, and she had skills I'd never learned, like tying knots.

So, I headed back down the driveway, armed with a coil of stiff yellow nylon rope, a slip-noose tied in its end. My mother tagged along, just in case she could help.

Fortunately, the rope was so stiff that I could work the noose under the dog's head without touching him. No chance of getting him back up onto the driveway—it had to be cross-country, through berry and grape vines, and the occasional scrubby bush of poison oak.

Dragging him was harder than I'd thought that it would be—his body caught on every clump of vegetation. I used all of my strength to pull on the rope—the noose tightened. I wrapped the rope around my wrists for better leverage, and tried to not think about what I was doing. Sweat poured down my forehead, stinging my eyes. I hadn't touched him, but I still didn't want to touch my face.

Out at the road at last, I looked down at him with sadness and relief. I considered the coil of rope in my hands, and called to my mother to bring me some scissors. I didn't want to have anything to do with rope that had touched the dog, but the rest of it—far too much to waste. So, I chopped it off at a thrifty length from his body, and went back down the driveway, ready to start the day anew, but first, a very long shower.

***

I needed a lot of scrubbing to feel clean, and my clothes went in the 'contaminated by poison oak' box, for extra care later. But the episode was done and I'd never have to think about it again. Except, what was that sound out by the road? It was far too soon for Animal Control to complete its bargain. I drifted uneasily back down the driveway.

Noise, out there where I'd left the dog. Voices. A police car, no, two of them, radios crackling. A van—I squinted—something about the Humane Society painted on its side. Clumps of people conferring. What was going on?

Then I saw it, saw the picture I'd painted. That poor dead dog, the bright yellow noose dug deep into its neck. Did they think that someone had hanged him? Did they think he'd been dragged behind a car? Whatever they thought, it was ugly, and they were taking it seriously. For a moment, I thought of casually retreating to the house. *No, I've got to set the record straight.*

I gave myself a fast pep talk. *Okay, say what happened but don't sound defensive. Don't be too wordy, but make them understand. Don't show any sign that you even realize why they're here. That's a tall order.*

I strolled a little closer, making a mental note that my bare feet on the dirt driveway might reinforce the image of cluelessness that I wanted to create, even though I hadn't planned it that way. I waved my hand, said "Hi."

A sheriff strode over to me, his voice stern. "Do you know who this dog belonged to?"

"No, but I know how he got here."

Now I had his attention. I told the story, no extra words, as clear as I could make it. "And I dragged him from right over there." I turned and pointed, and noticed with satisfaction that there was a massive crushed trail through the brambles.

Growing up, I'd lived a solitary life, usually with family, no one else. You don't need to think about body language with family. Most of the time you know what they're going to say before they say it. So, the articles about body language that I'd read in magazines didn't have much meaning for me. But now as I talked to that sheriff, although his face stayed as stern as ever, with every word, every phrase I spoke, I could see his body relaxing, his relief growing, as he realized that this wasn't an ugly little crime scene that he had to investigate. This was simply a well-meaning idiot who did something without realizing the consequences.

He didn't ask me any questions. He didn't thank me. He didn't say anything reproving, either, probably thinking that it would be wasted on me. I waited to see if he had anything to add, and then drifted away, back up the driveway, feeling a mixture of embarrassment at the trouble I'd caused them, and amazement that I'd somehow learned a skill I'd never quite believed in.

Maybe I could know what strangers were thinking—some of the time, anyway.

AUTHOR BIOGRAPHIES

Marlys Collom attended SDSU where she pursued a major in Journalism and polished her creative writing under the instruction of Jay Linthicum and Simon Ortiz. Her narrative poems lay naked on the page her deepest emotions and memorialize her life experiences. Her poetry has appeared in *The San Diego Times Review, the Journal of Contemporary Poets, The San Diego Poetry Annual, Baseball Bard,* and *Classifieds-An Anthology of Prose Poems.*

Gerry Strong always loved art and books. Children's books were a way to add stories to her art. She has won awards for both art and design. She is creator of the *Pug Detective Charlotte* Series and helps others realize the joy of seeing their books published. She has spoken at writer's groups and when not at her computer, teaches yoga. Learn more at www.downdogpressbooks.com.

Judy Opdycke is an avid people watcher who writes award-winning stories. The sequel to her just-completed middle-grade novel is her latest project. Beware: she may be the person observing you from behind that tall chai latte at your local coffee shop, ready to write you into her next tale.

Michele Ivy Davis is a freelance writer and photographer whose stories and articles appear in various magazines, anthologies, and newspapers. Her young adult novel, *Evangeline Brown and the Cadillac Motel,* was published by Dutton (Penguin Group USA) and won national and international awards. Learn more at www.MicheleIvyDavis.com.

Charlie Wyatt, a former Vietnam Swift Boat skipper during the Vetnam War—has a deep love for the written word. A bookstore owner for over twenty years, he has written for publications as varied as *Chicken Soup for the Soul,* and *Away for the Holidays* (a journal of veterans' experiences). A popular Writers' Group facilitator, Charlie also has expertise about rare books and coins.

A child of the Great Depression, **R. Boyd Palmer,** has written poetry since his 'hormones kicked in.' As an actor, he has appeared on stage, screen and TV. He married the love of his life, only to lose her to cancer after fifty happy years. Some of his poems appearing here are excerpted from his homage, *Love Lyrics to Linda* to be published in 2019.

Peter Cruikshank lives in the world of present reality, as well as a fantasy world of his imagination. His epic Medieval-themed High-Fantasy series, *Dragon-Called,* and other works, prove he spends much time in the latter. He hopes his writing provides readers an enjoyable escape, even if fleeting. Learn more at www.PeterCruikshank.com.

Elisa Blaisdell has lived most of her life in the Southern California backwoods—a quiet and solitary life with a few surprises, such as nearly dying in a wildfire, and acquiring a large and boisterous family at age 48. Her fantasy novel, *The Song of Andiene,* was published in 2016; her poems have appeared in *San Diego Poetry Annual.*

Pete Peterson's quest for baseball's Hall of Fame ended when he could hit neither the fastball nor the curve. His writing has appeared in *The Dead Mule School of Southern Literature, Stoneslide Corrective, Charles Carter – A Working Anthology, Ravens Perch,* and other magazines, newspapers and publications. Visit him at: www.pete-peterson. squarespace.com.

After five decades of work, and three college degrees, **John E. (Gene) Michals** is now semi-retired. That means he's as busy as ever — doing things that don't pay well. John's experience includes about 20 years each of newspaper writing/editing and technical writing/editing — plus a couple of years as an Army officer, and several odd jobs along the way. Currently he's more involved in editing — and pleasure reading — than content creation, but he churns out short stories on an erratic basis. In this anthology, he gives a glimpse of his ***Dark Side.***

www.ingramcontent.com/pod-product-compliance
Lightning Source LLC
Chambersburg PA
CBHW020306150626
46552CB00022B/1764